Serenity

ILIAS VENEZIS

Serenity

Translated by
Joshua Barley

AIORA

Co-funded by the
Creative Europe Programme
of the European Union

Joshua Barley is a translator of modern Greek literature and writer. He read Classics at Oxford and modern Greek at King's College, London. His translation of Makis Tsitas' *God Is My Witness* is published by Aiora Press. *A Greek Ballad*, selected poems of Michális Ganás (translated with David Connolly), is published by Yale University Press.

Original title: *Γαλήνη*

© Aiora Press 2019

ISBN: 978-618-5048-98-3

First edition May 2019
Reprinted July 2023

AIORA PRESS
11 Mavromichali St.
Athens 10679 - Greece
tel: +30 210 3839000
www.aiorabooks.com

Greeks lived in many parts of Asia Minor, or Anatolia, from the second millennium BC, when they settled all around the Mediterranean and the Black Sea. Greek culture flourished in Asia Minor and the Levant over the subsequent millennia, through the succession of empires that ruled the region. During the Byzantine Empire (330 AD–1453 AD), Greek language and culture prevailed, before the region came under the Ottoman Turks for the next four centuries. In the early 19th century, following the War of Independence against the Ottomans, the modern Greek state was born. Following other uprisings in the Balkans, and ultimately the First World War, the Ottoman Empire collapsed. In 1919, Greek forces, authorised by the Allies, were sent to the west coast of Asia Minor to protect the local Greek population, but faced immediate opposition. In the conflict that ensued—the Greco-Turkish War—the Greek forces won early victories but were ultimately defeated by the Turkish army under Mustafa Kemal, with dire consequences for the local civilian population. This calamity, culminating in the burning of the predominantly Greek port city of Smyrna (modern Izmir), is known in Greece as the 'Asia Minor Catastrophe'. Thus, after more than forty centuries of Greek presence in Asia Minor, one and a half million Greeks fled to Greece —which then had a population of only four million. The fledgling state struggled to cope with this influx.

PART ONE

CHAPTER ONE

Summer 1923: a multitude of Greek refugees from the East seek their new land in the wilderness of Anavyssos.

This story begins in July 1923. Anavyssos is a desolate place on the shores of the Saronic Gulf, roughly ten miles from Cape Sounion. No public road leads there. All the roads skirt the low hills that enclose this barren land, where the traveller will not find a single tree for shade. Lentisk, thorns, rushes and sand are all there is. The land has remained untilled for centuries, so that the sand, rain and sun have performed their works without the sweat of man. The hills continue down to the sea, girdling it and forming a natural bay with a narrow throat. Through this opening the jackals, hares and hornets can see the serene line of Aegina, Hydra and the Peloponnese in the distance, and who knows what they say among themselves about those far-flung lands.

For the traveller approaching from behind the hills, one single footpath leads to the seashore. The path finishes at the salt pans, the only sign of human life in this wilderness. The soil is heavy with clay, the succession of hills creates currents of air that draw away the clouds, and the salt dries easily in the pans, forming pyramids, white and tragic monuments of silence.

In a difficult year, when the rains do not favour the Mediterranean vines, the villagers living behind the hills take this path with their families, seeking work in the salt pans to survive. Some succeed, others are beaten to the work by those from more destitute parts, and still others cannot withstand the fevers brought on by the marshy waters of the small plain. This generation will pass, the next will come along, and then the next, all in turn taking the path to the sea when hunger pinches. That is how this path was made—a solid construction of the needy.

One morning in July 1923 the meltemi was not blowing as it usually does in the Saronic Gulf at that season. On one of the bare hills of Anavyssos, two people were digging, naked to the waist and dripping with sweat. Below them the sea was shimmering in the sun. The air was close and hazy, and the water in the pans was so stagnant that it was itself a reflection of the time and place.

'I'm exhausted,' said one of the two. 'This blasted heat!'

The other laid down his pickaxe.

'So am I, Vassilis, I'm sick of it. Where's this heading?'

'Let's be patient,' said the first. 'If we're lucky, it'll be our salvation!'

'If we're lucky, yes! But now we're starving while the others are making ends meet.'

He pointed down to the still salt pan.

'I think,' he continued, 'we should go down there too. I'm sick of this!'

The other did not want to give in.

'We've been digging for a month. You think we should give up just like that? Anyway, the statue must be somewhere here. Green said so. And when we find it...'

He did not complete his thought, as they had spoken about it so often.

'Are you sure,' said the other, 'that he'll pay you the right price? Remember what happened with the woman they found three years ago...'

Yes, he remembered what had happened three years ago. Other villagers had found that beautiful *kore* with the closed eyelids, fondly preserved by the earth for three thousand years. Green had taken her from them for peanuts. But were it not for him, they would have had to give her to the authorities, again for nothing. They later read in the newspapers of the vast sum the smuggler had made from sending the statue to America.

As they were talking, one of them noticed in the distance a cloud of dust rising at the furthest point of the footpath, where it met the hills.

'Look!' he said with surprise. 'What's that?'

'A herd of goats, surely?'

He disagreed. 'No herd would be on the path at this time. They're people.'

'People? Here? So many? The salt pans are full. What'll they do?'

'Just look! Look!'

They shielded their eyes from the sun. The great cloud rose higher, coming nearer. It was like a living substance, cautiously threading its way through the hills into this still landscape, silently making for the only friendly outlet—the sea—with the instinct of an animal.

'It's like an army!' said one of the villagers, even more startled. 'But no!' he corrected himself, 'I can see women and children.'

They looked at each other in fear. What were they after—with women and children too—in the wilderness of Anavyssos? Had an earthquake destroyed villages and forced the people to take the path to the sea in desperation?

'Let's go down quickly and look!'

'Yes, let's!'

The long procession came nearer. The cloud of dust lengthened in the close air and, little by little, was absorbed into it, mingling and disappearing with the adaptability possessed by things of this world. Beneath the cloud, however, the assimilation was not so easy. A multitude of women, children and old men were groaning loudly, embattled by the sun and the exhaustion of the journey. Dust, worked into the sweat on their faces, dripped like mud. The young men were few. Most of the crowd were barefoot, and all of them carried a load on their shoulders—a full sack or a bundle.

'Oh! Where have they sent us to live?' cried one woman. 'It's a desert here! A desert!'

Then the other women, taking their lead from her, began to wail and curse their fate.

'We'll die in this wild place! We'll die, along with our children! We'll die!'

The men, young and old, did what they could to abate the panic. Each one fought to calm the woman —his wife or mother—beside him. But the despair coursed through the thick air, fertile as pollen.

'Nothing…!' they wailed. 'Nothing will save us! This is our end!'

They cried out for a tree, just one tree under which they could find shade. But in the whole expanse of the small plain there was not one vertical line. The land was darkened only by lentisk, on which the sun shivered.

At that difficult hour came the misery of the water. When they set out from Kalyvia, the last inhabited place in the area, they had been told they would find two wells on the path, and then another near the sea. Having drunk at the first, they made for the next. The expectation of it appeased their terrible thirst and brought light to their hearts.

Then from the vanguard came the news: 'It's dry! The well is dry!'

Incapable of battling their fate any longer, they sat down on the ground. The cloud raised by their bloody feet halted above them. A deep moan passed through this yellow veil, struggling up towards God.

'What have we done?' they cried. 'What have we done to deserve this?'

Gradually their voices weakened until they were nothing but low groans.

Soon they heard the footsteps of one of their companions, who had gone ahead and was returning.

'Get up! Get up! The sea!' he cried.

The sea! Where? The fallen mass stirred as one, as a wave propelled by this friendly image and the extraordinary power of words.

'Get up! Get up!' shouted the men. 'One more push! We've reached the sea!'

The cloud, which had sunk onto the people, filled its sails again and moved with them like a boat in the sky. They ran downwards, skirting a low rise. A young voice, more fervent and violent than the rest, rang out, only to be dissolved in the dust: 'Salt! Salt! Look down there!'

The white pyramids in the salt pans—motionless, expressionless monuments—were glimmering in the silence of the horizon, and the light. Nothing could be more motionless and expressionless in this arid landscape. For these people, however, the pyramids cast a spell that sailed on the waves and over the mountains to their distant homeland, where salt pyramids whitened just like these.

It was a sudden, joyous stirring of memory, a distant message from the land that had raised them.

'Thank you, Lord!' they cried. 'At least there's that'— and they pointed to the salt.

Just then the two villagers approached from the hill.

'Hey, you there! Wait a moment!' they shouted to the crowd.

The crowd halted.

'Where are you going?'

'Is this not Anavyssos here?' a voice answered. 'We're coming here!'

'Who are you?'

'We are refugees.'

'And what are you looking for here?'

'We were given the land!' answered a voice from the crowd. 'We are going to live here!'

'The land? What land?' said one of the villagers in surprise. 'Only rushes grow in this land.'

And then, 'You'll die,' he told them, 'you and your children! You'll die, if you are really coming to live here!'

But the crowd, driven on now by the sight of the salt, continued down to the shore with its last ounce of strength.

The two villagers stopped short, watching the procession.

'And now?' said the first to recover from the shock. 'Now…?'

'Do you really think they'll stay?' asked the other.

'Didn't you see how desperate they are? They'll stay alright!'

With this assertion they realised at once what the news meant: if the refugees took the land, all this mystical labour, this struggling for ancient tombs, would be lost for good.

'The wretched people!' one of them cursed. 'They'll take the land we're digging! If they find out what we're up to, you can count on them to turn us in. Just when we had some hope…'

'We must inform *him*!' said the other. 'Let's go tonight!'

CHAPTER TWO

Two people completely alone: a woman and a man

When the refugees arrived on the shore, they finally found a few pine trees. The god of the place, who bestowed only barrenness, had driven the trees to grow at the foot of the low mountain, where the sea met the southern end of the ring of hills. They also found the brackish water of a well. When they had drunk, they lay down in the shade of the pines and groaned for many hours until, one by one, they fell silent. Evening closed in, serene. The lines of the mountains appeared clearer and the sea became calm. In the distance, a small island emerged.

'What island do you think that is?' someone asked.

'What does it matter to you?' came a bitter reply. 'It's a barren place, like this whole country. This place will be our tomb.'

A woman sighed and nodded assent. An old man sitting in silence was the only one to react, drawing on his experience: 'Don't be downcast, son! We'll get water and crops out of this earth, you'll see.'

Moved by similar feelings, two other members of the crowd were trying to find a way to speak, to soften the bitterness of this July evening. They had withdrawn from the others and were resting under a tree, the closest to the sea and slightly detached from the rest.

The man was about sixty. A white shock of hair and great blue eyes sat on top of a wiry body. The woman was young: she could easily have been his daughter. On her face, exhaustion in its harsh, dark tones was still as sallow light. Her eyes, which remained fixed on the sea as she leaned against the tree trunk, looked as though they were expecting a sinister enemy to spring up in front of them.

'Are you looking at the island, Irini?' the man asked hesitantly, searching for something to say.

She did not turn her face, but kept looking into the distance.

'It must be Hydra,' said the man. 'And over there, that will be the Peloponnese.'

Then, immediately: 'Yes, the island must be Hydra.'

He waited for a word of response.

'And that mountain we can see through the bay, that must be Aegina,' he continued. 'See how we've returned! These waters draw us back.'

For the entirety of the Great War, hounded from their native land, they had found refuge on Aegina. From there they witnessed the destruction of the world. Who would have thought that a few years later they would end up far from home again, this time for good, on the other shore?

'These waters draw us back…' said Dimitris Venis, the doctor.

The woman still said nothing.

'Say something, won't you!'

Then, lowering his voice, he asked her, 'Are you suffering a lot?'

'Please, Dimitris, don't put me through this…' she said, turning to him at last.

'I'm only asking, Irini, in case you need something. Do you want to lie down? I will take care of it.'

'Oh, of course you will! You'll take care of it!' Indignation flashed across her pale face.

'Why are you being unfair?' the man said, trying to calm her. 'You saw that we couldn't live in the city.'

A foreign, insignificant doctor, they say, is more useless than the last person on earth; he cannot put food on the table and he is too proud to beg.

'And what's going to happen to us here? We'll die of hunger and pride!'

'Don't say that!' protested the doctor. 'Our lives will change, you'll see. We will live with the people of our homeland and help them, and they won't abandon us.' A moment later, he added hesitantly, 'Besides… this… there is some small purpose in this.'

She looked daggers at him.

'Oh, you and your small purposes! I've been hearing about them ever since I married you. I'm sick of it. I've had enough!'

Dimitris Venis kept trying, in his mild way, to make her see reason. Was he to blame if he could not? Was he to blame for their suffering?

'We're refugees,' he said. 'Am I to blame?'

Night fell gradually over the hills and the sea. The voices of the crowd, scattered under the trees, began to gather strength. All were trying to make themselves comfortable for their night's sleep. They lit a few fires.

'I'm going to look for water,' said the doctor.

He took a jug from their sack and made for the well. When he returned he did not find his wife at the tree. He called softly for her.

'Irini! Irini!'

'She didn't come this way, Doctor,' answered a male voice. 'She went towards the sea.'

Then the same voice: 'Can I help you with something?'

No, he did not want anything. Everyone must look after themselves.

He looked around at the fires they had lit.

Should we light one too? he wondered. The nights are bound to be chilly.

He decided to wait for his wife to come back.

'What'll become of her, poor miserable thing?' he said to himself. 'It's difficult, but who can be blamed?'

He heard footsteps approaching. He recognised them.

'Is that you?'

'Yes.'

'Here, I've fetched water. We can eat what we have left. Do you want to light a fire?'

'I do not want anything,' she said wearily.

'It's just one night,' the doctor said. 'Tomorrow they will send tents. But it might be cold. I think—if you want—I should gather some branches for a fire.'

'Don't worry,' the woman said. 'I will stay up all night.'

'As you wish…'

His voice showed his exhaustion, and the effort he was making to endure the suffering.

The stars had now come out. There was no moon. The night settled on the hills and the gentle waves.

Then, out at sea in the opening of the bay, a brightly lit procession appeared, passing slowly over the waves through the night.

'Look…' murmured Irini Venis. 'Look down there…'

The light of a boat was travelling past. Before it disappeared behind the headland, another appeared in the same spot, then another, and another.

'I wonder where they are going,' the woman said to herself.

'To the Cyclades, perhaps. They leave from Piraeus in the evening.'

Another boat joined the procession. It was very large and its lights shone even brighter. The low rumble of its engines sounded clear and strange.

'That one must be going further.'

'Yes, it might be.'

The other people who were still awake suddenly saw the magic of the sea. Small voices rang out from under the trees: 'Look over there! Look there!'

Incandescent, relentless and unwavering, the life of the world disappeared in the watery distance. And here was a multitude of displaced people who had to bind themselves together and put down roots with the blind instinct of a plant. How strange the other world looked out there, slipping away into the night.

The last lights in the distance were vanishing when Dimitris Venis heard her sob next to him.

He leaned over her.

'Don't cry, Irini,' he said gently. 'God won't abandon us.'

He placed her head carefully in his lap.

'It's nothing,' she answered, trying to hold herself together.

'I'm cold,' she said after a while, trembling.

He pulled a blanket over her.

She huddled her legs up. That seemed to do some good.

'Are you still cold?' he asked her a short time later.

There was no reply.

She must be asleep, he thought.

He looked around. Almost no sound came from the trees of the others, only a little moaning. A chill descended, but Dimitris Venis had the feeling that the tree overhead kept them from danger. His body sensed that outside the tree's protection the darkness was a dense, wet mass. At the far end of the bay there were no more boats. The procession had finished. In the northern sky the Great Bear travelled on, indifferent, certain.

Then, on that damp night in the Saronic Gulf, Dimitris Venis, a sixty-year-old man of this world, brought before him one by one the years that had gone by—strange boats that sailed through the air like birds.

CHAPTER THREE

The message of the fire

The same night, high above the campsite of the refugees, on Prophet Elijah—the highest mountain of the region—an old man was looking towards the sea. The mountain is inhabited by a few families of hut-dwelling Arvanites.[1] Their homes, made of earth and sticks, are not easily visible in the landscape. They pasture their flocks here all year, only taking them for a few months in the summer to Mount Parnitha. When their time comes they will be buried on the mountain of Anavyssos, and so will their children, and their children's children: so it goes from generation to generation. They wear clothes woven by their women, made from their animals' wool. They eat cheese and meat of their animals, and grain that they have sown on mountainsides cleared by their hands. The serenity of the mountain, the solidity of its bulk, and the imper-

---

[1] Ethnic Albanians who have lived in Greece for centuries.

turbability of their fate is written on their faces and in their movements.

On that July night of 1923, one of the Arvanites, an elder, was sitting on a rock and looking at the stars. By day the whole of the Saronic Gulf could be seen from there—Cape Sounion, San Giorgi, Aegina, Makroniso, Hydra and the boats travelling past. At night, though the islands and the sea and the lines cannot be seen, they exist in memory even more clearly, even more *visibly*.

The old man was surrounded by the noises of the land, by all the days that had gone by and the few that remained until he returned to the earth. He looked absent-mindedly down towards the shore of Anavyssos.

All of a sudden he thought he could make out a fire. Soon another was lit, then another and another.

No, I must be wrong, he thought. It cannot be anything.

He rubbed his eyes with his hands, but the fires remained, grew stronger, then died down.

'Oh!' said the old man, uncomprehending. 'What is it?'

He could not remember such a thing happening his whole life. Now and then fishermen working on boats between Sounion and Fleves would light fires on land to make their fish soup. But such small fires could not be seen from above.

'Is it an army?'

He knew it could not be. What would an army be doing there?

Suddenly the unshakeable man, surrounded by the emptiness and the night, quivered with fear. It came skulking slyly into his blood: an ancient, ancestral fear, from the times when pirates ravaged the salt pans and the sheepfolds.

He felt as feeble as a reed. Standing up, he cupped his hands around his mouth and bleated into the night, 'Ey! Ey! Ey!'

The mountain took the call, casting it onto the slopes and bringing it down the other side, to his son and family.

'Ey! Ey! Petrooooos!' he shouted again, with all his might, and listened for a response.

From the other side a voice returned quickly, asking what was wrong.

'Come up!' the old man shouted. 'Come quickly!'

'Has something happened?'

'Come and look!'

He waited for his son to reach the summit.

'What's happened, Father?' he asked, still some way off.

The old man pointed down at the fires.

'Look!'

'Oh!' exclaimed the young man, taken aback. 'What is it?'

'I don't know. But we must find out!'

'What could it be?'

'So many fires together cannot bode well!'

The young man looked for a way to quell their unease.

'Many or few, what's it to us? They'll go.'

The old man, however, carried with him the wisdom of his years.

'If there were few, maybe. But there are many, so many that they must have some purpose here. They'll stay. Understand?'

He understood. It spelt disaster for them and their flocks if there were other people on their nurturing land. His mind wandered momentarily. What if they were destitute and had come to work on the salt pans? But if that were so, they would have been billeted in the sheds.

'We must give the news to the others!' said the old man. 'Tonight!'

At that moment another voice rang out from far off. They listened. Shouts were coming from the other huts.

'Ey! Ey! Did you see the fires at Anavyssos?'

'Ey! We saw them!'

'What are they?'

'Send word to the other huts below! Meet at Prophet Elijah at dawn!'

From slope to slope the voice brought the message of the fire.

CHAPTER FOUR

Irini Venis, the fairy tale of the East and a wild bird

Dawn broke. It was a serene day of perfect stillness, of the kind that occurs in this land, as if the elements of the world—the air, the clouds—have all been drawn away.

The first noises emerged from the camp: people conversing beside a tree, the voices of a couple of children.

A woman cautiously approached the pine tree where the Venis couple had settled. Irini was sleeping with her head resting on her husband's legs. He had woken up. He seemed to be cold still: he had draped a blanket over his shoulders. When he saw the woman approaching, he signalled her to be quiet.

'Shhh,' he said, pointing at his wife. 'She's asleep.'

The woman came closer.

'Is there nothing you want?' she asked him.

'No, nothing, Eleni. But if you want, come later to help her.'

She went away, treading as lightly as when she had come.

She was barefoot and dressed in black. A woman of the people. Her round face was deathly pale and even though she was still young, wrinkles lined her cheeks and forehead.

At the tree to which she returned, a little girl was sitting down, holding a sleeping baby.

'Where's your brother?' Eleni asked the girl.

'I don't know, Mother. I think he went to the beach.'

'Ah, to the beach!' she fumed. 'Is that where he's got to? Go and get him!'

She took the baby from the girl's arms, put her down and covered her with a blanket. When the girl made to leave, however, she stopped her.

'Oh, let your brother play, Zabeta,' she said with regret. 'Go and fetch some water instead.'

Zabeta had clear blue eyes and blonde hair that was still full of dust from the journey. Her face had an unnatural solemnity for her age, and her small body was bent as if from a heavy weight.

'Can I go to the beach too, Mother?' she pleaded.

'Oh, you too? No, you will help me! Don't you pity me at all?'

With that she put the jug in her daughter's hands.

When the girl left, the woman bent down and started clearing stones. 'She'll have caught a cold,' she said to herself, thinking of Irini Venis. 'Poor lady, it's difficult for you.' Eleni is alone and thinks only of the hardships of others, perhaps to feel her own less keenly. 'And how is he to blame?' she says of Dimitris.

'Such a good, mild person! It's just they weren't meant to live together. It wasn't fated. And now that this great misfortune has arrived…'

Irini Venis was separated from the other refugees by an impenetrable wall. Her family were once nobility. That gave a tragic element to her present decline, and it is not only in the ancient tragedies that the chorus weeps. 'Oh, poor lady!' continued the woman of the people. 'How harsh your fate has been!'

And while she bent down to the ground to clear around the tree that was their home, her own hardship left on the slight breeze that blew off the gulf, so that only the hardship of the other woman was left.

She remembered Irini Venis as a girl in their homeland, with the great house and garden, in the carriage —the phaeton—when she was taken for her evening promenade. Her father was the British consul. He had a *kavass*,[2] a fearfully tall black African, who always sat beside Irini in the phaeton, wearing a flamboyant costume with gold buttons. Those trips were wonderful as a fairy tale, with the guard, and the little princess gazing earnestly from her moving throne at the children, women and fishermen who gathered to look as she passed. The *kavass* was by far the most epic element of the fairy tale. The women used him to frighten their children into going to sleep. They could never under-

---

[2] A Turkish word for an armed consular guard.

stand how such a small and fragile child as Irini was not afraid of him. They would see him whisking her down from the carriage, her entrusting herself entirely to him, tugging at his moustache while he laughed and let his two lovely rows of teeth gleam.

When Irini reached a certain age, she spent her winters in the city. She studied there, near her older sister Maria, who lived there with her husband. Irini only returned in summer, always wearing a white dress. The *kavass* would lift her out of the boat and onto the quay, where the women and children of the village were waiting, surrounding the honourable representative of His Royal Highness.

'Which young local lad could Irini take when her time comes?' the women asked, and all agreed there was no young man in these parts fit for her. Irini herself had said one day, 'A young prince will come from afar on a boat, and he'll carry me off!'

Fate, however, laid its merciless hand on their house. The old consul had suddenly been ruined by land guarantees he had given in a year when the land produced no crops. The great house was sold to the creditors; the phaeton lost its horses. Only the *kavass* remained, trailing on foot behind his master and Irini on their long lonely walks outside the city. They took down the two lions from the coat of arms on the door of their house. One winter, some years before the Great War in Europe, the old consul lost his life when the boat on which he was travelling to Smyrna was shipwrecked. Thus, from all the ornaments of the fairy tale, by the end all that was left was the *kavass* with his gold-buttoned uniform and its faded colours. Old, silent and wretched, he wandered the streets until the earth claimed him back.

It was then that the doctor, Dimitris Venis, appeared in their small city. What was he doing there? He came from Isparta in the Anatolian hinterland, a place where they speak Turkish and cultivate roses. He was twice Irini's age when he sought her hand in marriage. At first, it was said, she steadfastly refused to give herself to such an old man from foreign lands. Was this the 'prince with the boat' of her childhood? But there was no other hope. In the end she went with him—the girl with the phaeton and the gold-buttoned *kavass*.

After that she turned in on herself, bottled herself up, became estranged from everyone and everything. She avoided people, spoke rarely, and pretended to be a woman devoted to her house, happy and alone. It was a reaction born of her humiliation, and a way of hiding her panic. Gradually she cut herself off from everyone. The local women would whisper behind her back about how haughty she was. By the time their first and only child was born she had grown accustomed to her fate. She had nothing in common with Dimitris Venis. Yet he had shown her such devotion from the start that imperceptibly, as the years went by, she managed to set aside this humiliation. Gradually she became used to the fantasies of this strange, weak man, who had such grand plans and visions and admired power wherever he saw it.

'I've got it! Hot off the press!' he said lovingly, piously opening the small packet: a biography of Napoleon Bonaparte.

'Ah,' she said sarcastically, 'the one who gambled the earth in an hour or two, and lost it all at Waterloo', reminding him of a silly poem he loved.

'It contains completely new material!' he assured her, without noting her sarcasm.

That night he dived passionately into the unread pages on which the epic days of the nineteenth century played out, while his young wife slept beside him. She would fall asleep and then, startled awake by the light, would find him completely absorbed in reading, with bloodshot eyes and his face pale with emotion.

'Won't you finally go to sleep?' she said. 'Your patients will be expecting you in the morning.'

'Oh, it's wonderful!' he replied, not hearing her advice. 'The days on Saint Helena...'

On those sleepless winter nights, there would occasionally be a sudden knock on the door from someone seeking help for an invalid. He would leap up frantically and go out into the rain and the storm to help, driven by his visions of power, believing that he himself was doing something grand and powerful. He would return home after a while, sodden, filthy, almost brimming with joy.

'What extraordinary weather!' he would say to his wife triumphantly. 'The storm is raging outside!'

'Is there hope?' she asked, believing his joyous note had something to do with the invalid.

'I don't think so...' he would say, forced to change tone suddenly. 'But... well... *I* battled with the storm and with the will of the Highest.'

Once and once only did there arise the possibility of something remarkable happening in his own life, an epic page being written. In the first days of the Great War of 1914, before the uprooting, a felucca left the closest shore of Chios and took a man at night to a remote corner of their land. The man went into town, saw the elders and received information in secret.

The Turks captured this Greek the moment he was departing for Chios, and took all his papers. The next day, the early risers in the town saw three corpses twirling from the great branches of a plane tree. All three were elders who governed the community. A note was placed on each man's chest, condemning them as traitors.

Dimitris Venis returned home that morning silent and grave. He shut himself in his room and waited alone for many hours. By that time he was also an elder.

When he came out of his room, Irini was staring at him.

'Put on a black dress,' he said, 'and come with me.'

His voice had a strange, unusually commanding tone.

He took her down to the scene. A great crowd had gathered. It was drizzling. The wind was coming off the open sea, rocking the hanging bodies.

'Are you afraid?' asked Dimitris.

Her face was ashen, but she did her utmost to keep herself together.

'No,' she replied, squeezing his hand.

They went home in silence.

'You must remember this, to be brave,' said Dimitris. 'That is why I brought you.'

'I will remember.'

He believed in Greece, in the great dreams of the race. All the fairy tales he told Anna, their daughter, sailed in that distant, beloved Greece: much light blue; much blood; the wind ruffling the hair of a youth from foreign lands, drawn by its call and killed on the sacred earth; women dancing arm in arm, one by one, into the abyss.[3]

'They're sailing to Greece too,' he muttered to himself about the hanged elders, when he and his wife returned home. 'Remember them in your prayers tonight, Irini.'

The next evening, Dimitris Venis went home more solemn and pensive. The Turks had not stopped interrogating people about the incident. They seized

---

[3] This is a reference to the 'Dance of Zalongo', when a group of Greek women danced off a cliff to avoid capture by the Ottoman ruler Ali Pasha in 1803.

several women, to force their husbands to confess. Dimitris felt the net closing around him.

'Listen, Irini!'

He looked at her in such a way that the young woman began to tremble.

'I don't know,' he said to her, 'but they might take me too. We need to prepare ourselves.'

He gave her instructions about household matters, handed her the keys and showed her the papers. The night was well advanced.

'After me, they might try to take you too,' he said, and looked at her with serenity and assurance. 'I know that you will be brave whatever happens. You're a Greek woman!'

She took his hands and kissed them, her whole body shaking with emotion.

Then the Venis couple withdrew to their room, lowered the light and waited.

No one came. Not that night, nor the next. No one. The epic page remained blank.

Nonetheless, that episode played its part. And time did so too, placing a layer of affection in the proud heart of the woman and bringing her closer to him. Indeed, one might even have predicted a calm end to their lives, a final reconciliation and serenity. But the tide turned in the world outside, violently shaking a balance that had been established with great effort.

The persecution of the Christian populations of the Greek East and the region's subsequent destruction did not only deprive them of their property, it also struck them deeper. It revealed the void and stripped it bare.

. . . .

The chorus also perceived the new workings of the times. It ceased to see the 'haughty' woman with anger. It saw more clearly the proud beast who, struck down again, fell into the mud.

'Oh, poor lady!' continued Eleni, the peasant woman. 'How harsh your fate is!'

She looked silently at the fallen, huddled, grubby body sleeping at the foot of the tree.

The body stirred. The sun was already quite high. Irini opened her eyes.

'Oh, is that you, Eleni?'

'I've come to help you, m'lady. I'll boil some water and you can have camomile tea. It'll do you good. Where's the doctor?' she asked, lighting a fire.

Irini shrugged.

'He'll have gone to the other trees to see if anyone needs anything.'

'Oh, what a saint he is, m'lady,' said Eleni, with genuine feeling, 'to come and live with us in this desert! Who else would have done it? How indebted we are to him—us and our children!'

'Of course no one else would have done it,' grumbled Irini bitterly to herself.

Realising that she was giving away her feelings, however, she sealed her lips.

'Will your daughter stay permanently in Athens, then?' asked Eleni.

'She'll stay as long as is necessary,' Irini replied tersely.

The remembered image of her child appeared clearly in the space between the two women on that serene Attic morning: her serious face the colour of wheat, her curls dark and her eyes bright.

'Oh, that girl is your spitting image, m'lady!' said Eleni admiringly. 'You were just like that, back then, with the *kavass*…'

The words stung. Irini Venis looked at her severely: 'Quiet! Enough!'

Eleni withdrew, startled.

'I didn't mean anything, m'lady,' she excused herself respectfully. 'Just please don't be so bitter about it all…'

Meanwhile, she had prepared tea.

'Come on, m'lady, drink this,' she said kindly. 'It'll do you good.'

She spoke to her with the same respect—calling her 'm'lady'—as she had when the family was flourishing and she was their servant. She had grown up in the great house of the consul until she married Fotis Glaros, and she would not think of abandoning that detachment now in their shared disaster.

Irini drank the tea. It did indeed do her good. She raised her head and looked around her. At the end of the small bay, where it opened out, stood the gleaming white church of St Nicholas. Her gaze followed the line of the bay. She saw a mountain, green with pines marching down to the sea. It was not, in fact, one mountain, but three successive hills cutting off the land to the north. Well, there are trees, she thought, even if they are far away. Her gaze fell intently on that spot. Eleni, stirred by its power, turned to see what was there.

There was nothing other than the mountains. Then suddenly a sign appeared in the sky: a bird, high up, coming nearer.

'Look at that bird,' Irini said, startled. 'How black it is…'

'It's a hawk, m'lady. It's not black.'

Then, as if she sensed the fear trembling in Irini's gaze, she said, 'It's just a bird. It's nothing.'

The hawk passed slowly over the salt pan and its pyramids, came above them, drew a great circle and disappeared behind the mountain.

'Oh!' Irini breathed a sigh of relief. 'What did I think it was?' she said to herself. 'It was just a bird.'

She got up and shook out her hands. Her whole body felt numb. Dimitris was approaching.

'Ah, well done!' he said, seeing she was up. 'You are feeling alright, then?'

'Yes.'

'I've been around all the trees. Everyone is fine. I think it's a good place. I'm just concerned there are swamps.'

'No need to be concerned,' said his wife drily. 'Whether there are or not, we're staying here.'

He did not notice—or pretended not to notice—her sarcasm.

'Certainly we'll stay, and we will cover them if there are any.'

'And of course you will be at the head of this heroic deed!'

'You are not being kind,' he said. 'We had to come here. Now we need to get back on our feet.'

'Oh, I have no doubt! No, there was nowhere else we could get back on our feet other than here…'

He had nothing else to say. Eleni brought him some camomile tea.

'I'll leave now, but I'll be back,' she said. 'Call me if there is anything you want.'

The two of them were alone again.

'Will we sleep under a tree again tonight?' she asked indifferently. The firm tone she had taken when Eleni was there yielded slightly.

'They promised that the tents would come by boat today. They cannot be lying. I hope you don't have to suffer again tonight,' he said.

There was a small commotion in the refugee camp. People stood up, pointing towards the gorge between the two hills.

'Look! People are coming! Who are they?'

It was a procession of fifteen or twenty Arvanites, young and old, with sunburnt faces, capes on their backs and crooks in their hands. They approached with silent formality, figures emerging from the depths of history. Their slow pace and silence scattered an intangible fear among the crowd of Phocians.[4]

Everyone congregated unconsciously in the same place, in the middle of their camp, as if to gather together their strength.

'Good day!' said the first shepherd, a tall, old man, the most respected of them all, and the one whom the reader will remember on the mountain top the previous night. 'Good day!' he said, and cast his eyes around.

On his right and left and behind him stood the other shepherds, crooks nestled into their armpits.

'Welcome!' replied many of the refugees.

'Who are you?' asked the old man slowly.

'We're refugees! Our homeland was Phocis!'

'And where have you come from now?'

'We have wandered the Peloponnese for a year and suffered greatly. Now we have been given the land here, to live on.'

A ripple passed through the planted crooks of the shepherds. They shifted a little, then became still again. No one other than the old man spoke.

'You have been given this land, you say?' His voice had become gruff. 'Who gave it to you? What land?'

'The state said to us, "The land of Anavyssos is yours." We were told to come and take it.'

---

[4] The refugees came from Phocaea, a town just north of Izmir that had been settled by Greeks since ancient times.

'You were told to come and take it? And where are your flocks, your animals?'

'We have no flocks. We are not shepherds. We will clear the land, plant vines and sow wheat.'

'What are you talking about, imbecile, planting wheat and vines in this land?' the old man cried furiously. 'Look over there!'

He raised his staff and traced a circle around the whole of the small plain enclosed by the hills. All eyes followed involuntarily, yielding to the commanding gesture.

'Since we have been here,' he said rudely, 'and our fathers and their fathers too, only rushes and bracken have grown here, and no other living thing besides our flocks! So, what wheat and vines do you mean?'

He had the grave, indissoluble and pitiless air of ancient things, of fate and death, and his deep voice emerged from the depths of time to defend the land against barbarians.

'Only us and our flocks, I tell you, can survive in this desolate land. That's how we received it from our forefathers! We alone can endure it here. The earth calls to us and commands us! What are you after, you wretches, in our lands?'

His voice trembled as he spoke, foreseeing that his efforts would be in vain.

'You'll die of thirst!' he said. 'There's no well here. And if you dig deep and strike a vein, the water will be brackish from the sea. Fevers, wind and sand will strike you down. If a crop grows, the sand will settle on its leaves and wither it. Before you see a harvest you'll be dead, you and your children. So, get out of here!'

Stonily, gruffly, savagely, he repeated, 'Get out of here!'

He fell silent and lowered his staff, his eyes piercing the crowd of Phocians.

A murmur passed through the refugees. The voice of the land, speaking through the old man, his terrible words, the vision of terrible and certain death that he cast over them, had numbed them and scattered fear among them—a dark cloud in a clear sky. They stood mutely like bare trees, bare roots waving blindly, tangling their tormented tentacles in the air, searching with plantlike instinct for earth.

They stood there until the wind, blowing off the Saronic Gulf, drew away the spirit of panic. Then, just as ferociously, with all the dark power of bodies trying to stabilise themselves, first one voice, then another, then all together, women and men, young and old, began to yell, 'We're not leaving! Never again! They gave us this land and we're staying! We're staying! We're staying!'

The wind took the voices and scattered them, striking them on the slopes of the mountain and strengthening them. A cloud of sand rose up, enveloping the people. They bellowed and waved their hands high in the hazy cloud, hazy themselves like beasts of the deep.

'We'll stay here even if we die! We'll stay here even if we die!'

Then the rage that was swelling among the Arvanites broke out.

'Very well!' cried the old man, and other shepherds with him. 'Stay then, and we'll see who this land supports! We'll strike you wherever we find you, we'll kill your animals if you have any, we'll trample your crops if they grow! You'll never find favour with us, nor with our children, until your seed is wiped out for good!'

Their fearsome voices rang on even after they had disappeared into the gorge whence they came.

Then the cloud of sand came down to rest on the earth. Silent, heavy-hearted, oppressed by the sharp wave of fear, the crowd of Phocians keeled over onto the ground.

CHAPTER FIVE

*In which a person tries to pursue wild fantasies
in the land of Anavyssos.*

The next day dawned slowly over the sleeping Phocians, who had spent a second night under the trees. In
the east, above the line of hills, the morning star was
hovering over the dry land of Anavyssos like a hawk
watching its prey.

Fotis Glaros woke up and nudged his wife, who was
sleeping next to him.

'Eleni!'

She woke with a start.

'Has something happened?' she said, getting up.

'No, nothing. It was a quiet night.'

'I was afraid the shepherds would trouble us. Thank
God!'

'I think we have nothing to fear for the moment.
But they'll get us later, mark my words!'

Like all of them, she had grown accustomed to
evaluating only the present moment. Future happiness
or unhappiness was a distant prospect.

'Who knows!' she said, and thanked God again for the peaceful night.

'I'll leave when the sun is fully up,' said Fotis. 'I'll go to look over the land. We'll need to choose our plot and make a start.'

'I don't know if there's any point in choosing,' the woman said. 'Every bit of land is as dry as the next. And…'

She stopped without finishing her thought. She knew her husband did not usually take her advice. She had learned, like her mother, to submit.

She merely asked, 'Do you want me to come with you?'

No, he did not. What could she do? She would have to take care of the children.

'I'll go alone.'

He was of short, weak build with small, intelligent eyes, and still very young. His veins stood out on his arms.

After more than five hours he returned, exhausted.

'It's as you say,' he said to his wife. 'The land is the same all over.'

'So we choose blindly?'

'Yes. Tomorrow I'll show you the place. It's nearby.'

They were silent for a moment. They did not have a clear sensation of what was happening, but somewhere deep down they felt a shadowy foreboding that this moment decided the fate of a small world that had not yet seen the light of day: the history of their children, wrapped in the history of the land they chose.

'It's close to God, though,' he said, referring to the place.

Fotis had walked around the dry plain and was returning, having decided to take any old plot, when he came upon a half-ruined chapel. It had no door, no icons. It was one of the humble refuges of Attica, used in Byzantine times by hermits—simple, God-fearing people who covered the walls with the spirit of their painful conflict with the environment, painting themselves in the manner of saints. Like the similar refuges on Mount Hymettus, the walls, hammered by centuries of wind and rain, showed nothing but a little colour and a few shapes; the rest had been sucked away by the weather.

Fotis crossed himself in front of the chapel.

'Help me!' he said to God. 'I have a wife and small children.'

He inspected the place and noticed many stones. There was also a very long, low wall. At first he took it for a field boundary. But upon closer inspection he saw how sturdily it was set in the earth, and concluded that it was the ruins of a building.

'People must have lived here once,' he said. 'Surely, then, it's better than the other parts of the plain?'

From the depths of time emerged the warmth of man, who had once tamed and blessed this earth with his toil. Fotis looked around. The sea was not more than half a mile away. And the streams, as he noticed from the drainage furrows, must run lower down. He need not, therefore, fear damage if it rained a lot.

'Here!' he said, and crossed himself.

'Have the others still not come back?' Fotis asked his wife, glancing at the trees.

'They must be looking for something.'

'What is there to look for?' he asked, for he now had an opinion about the land. 'Is the doctor also away?'

'No, I didn't see him leave. He's somewhere around.'

Fotis went to look for him.

He usually did what his instinct told him, having blind faith in the dark powers that haunt man. Nonetheless, precisely because of this—the feeling that his decisions were definitive and irreversible, answerable only to God—he understood the need to have the consensual opinion of another being. Very rarely was this other being his wife. She was a part of his very self; she should be another mouth for *his* voice, and hence could not be used for this purpose. The doctor, who was the world's wisdom among the refugees, was his surest support.

He continued towards their tree. Dimitris Venis and his wife were talking about the same thing. The group camaraderie, which had united them up until the day before, bound together as they were by the journey and the dangers of these foreign parts, had begun to weaken as each of them scattered to choose their land.

'All the men are away. Do you know why?' Dimitris Venis was saying to his wife.

'Yes,' she said, before adding brusquely, 'only *you* are here!'

He pretended not to notice, as he did a lot lately.

'I wouldn't have anything to do,' he said. 'What do I know about land? But I too have my plans…'

'What are they?' asked Irini indifferently.

He tried to show her how well things would turn out. There were a few trees around them. The sea was right there. They would make their village when the state helped them build their shacks. They could see the boats going by. It was calm. They would dig the earth at the foot of the mountain. The villagers would help them dig, and he would take care of their health.

She went along with it, showing no interest whatsoever.

'And then…' said Dimitris Venis, his voice becoming serious.

The change in tone made her turn her head.

'Yes?'

'And then, where we have cleared… I will plant roses,' he said, his voice trembling a little.

Irini wanted to laugh. But she stifled this urge and her face took its more customary sour expression.

'You've never done anything that wasn't useless and mediocre!' she said. 'There I was thinking that you would prepare the land—even if only this small piece you have chosen—for wheat. I thought you might do something positive and useful for once. But it seems you were destined to do the opposite, right to the end.'

Under the shade of the pine, her voice did not take any softness from the dew-cooled tree. It remained dry and pitiless.

'Yes, quite the opposite, right to the end,' she repeated harshly.

Dimitris, stung, raised his voice: 'Well, you're no different, and you'll never change!'

But he also wanted to explain himself to her. He told her that everyone in his homeland cultivated roses. Rose water was more profitable than wheat. All his ancestors cultivated roses. Only he had not followed the tradition. But now that he had been given the opportunity to revive a piece of land...

Just then Fotis arrived at their tree. Irini turned and saw him, determined to humiliate her husband.

'We're also going to cultivate the land, Fotis!' she said. 'Did you hear?'

'Have you chosen your plot?' he asked. 'Who chose the land for you?'

'We'll cultivate the land here at the foot of the mountain,' said Irini. 'We'll plant roses!'

She looked piercingly at the simple man, pleased at the surprise written on his face.

'We'll plant roses!' she repeated, with a note of sneering triumph.

'But that's impossible!' Fotis ventured, and a desire to laugh danced in his small eyes. 'How will you work this stony ground? And what will you do with the roses if they grow?'

'We'll wear them in our hair!' said Irini Venis, and her eyes lit up.

Her flashing eyes had the wildness of a wounded animal. Dimitris said nothing. He looked towards the sea, trying to restrain himself.

'On the plain there is land you can clear,' said Fotis. 'It'll be enough for all of us. That's where you should take your land, Doctor. You'll be able to plant vines, like us, and sow wheat.'

Dimitris turned slowly and looked at him. 'We'll stay here!' he decreed, before adding more quietly, 'God willing.' His weak and almost elderly voice had an improbable decisiveness.

A sky-blue line above the dust of the earth, containing trees and tombs, and flashes of lightning that are drawn, erased and plunged into the sea, and beyond everything the silence, the final boundary of the world—what, I wonder, is the fate of the world? Oh reader, I am trying to tell of the fate of a few people; I would like to tell of the bones the sea will cover and whiten after numberless years. And I know nothing more worthy of ridding man of the bitterness of uncertainty than the silence and certainty of the stars.

The life-giving earth crashed around in burning, and the vast wood crackled loud with fire all about. All the land seethed, and Ocean's streams and the unfruitful sea. The hot vapour lapped round the earthborn Titans: flame unspeakable rose to the bright upper air: the flashing glare of the thunderstone and lightning blinded their eyes for all that they were strong. Astounding heat seized Chaos...[5]

That is how it happened, in the great struggle for the harmony of the world. In the beginning was Chaos, then the broad Earth, then the power that drags bodies against each other so life can continue. Then night came, with light and the sky, the deity of movement and duration, the divinities of the rivers and springs.

Then a star said, 'Look down there, at Earth. I think it is moving.'

'It is indeed,' answered another star.

And the silence of the frozen firmament covered again the night and the deeps, at the beginning of human life on Earth.

It will be no different when the final hour comes.

---

[5] Hesiod, 'The Theogony' in Hesiod, the *Homeric Hymns and Homerica*, trans. Hugh G. Evelyn-White (London, New York: 1914), p. 693.

CHAPTER SIX

Tombs

Life began to run its usual course in Anavyssos. The state gave tents, tools and the meagre means for the refugees to build shacks and live until the earth they had cleared bore fruit.

From first light, the multitude of Phocians took the road to the fields. Only the sick and old stayed to keep watch over the settlement. They still feared the shepherds, though they had shown no sign of malice since the first day when they sent their envoys. The builders, who were constructing the shacks out of mud bricks, were also staying there.

Fotis was working with his family on his chosen land, next to the chapel. From time to time he would also go to another field he had been allotted, at Thymari.

The work was difficult, the fallow soil was hard and the place full of stones and lentisk. As the days went by, Fotis' wife became more and more concerned that they had not chosen a good place.

'I think we'll come up against rock,' she said to her husband.

Fotis stopped digging, realising where the conversation was heading.

'People lived here once,' he answered stubbornly. 'I know what I'm doing! We'll follow in their footsteps.'

Eleni said nothing and began to dig again. Her husband might be right. She certainly could not be sure that the earth here was any worse than the earth of the pieces of land their fellow countrymen had taken. And it was a consolation that they were treading on soil that, perhaps, others had once trodden on and worked before them.

The days went by until, one morning, Fotis' pickaxe fell upon a more certain indication of those people. A wall, made of enormous stones, appeared at a shallow depth.

'Come and look!' he called to his wife. 'Is this not a wall here?'

It certainly was. The two of them inspected it closely, noting its solid construction.

What was it? What was this world whose traces were emerging?

'The people in the salt pans, who know the land, say strange things,' said Fotis. 'They say that there was once a great civilisation and that a part of it sank into the sea.'

So they say. When there is no wind and all is calm, in the depths of the bay they can see walls, large earthenware jars and other works of human hand.

'It seems it was lost in the flood told of in the Gospel,' Fotis concluded.

'It might have been,' said his wife, running her hand over the huge stones of the wall. 'What kind of people lived there, I wonder?'

Fotis seemed to be thinking.

'Do you think these things have any value?' he pondered. 'In these parts they make much of the buried stones they find.'

His wife, however, was down-to-earth. Imagination is an exercise that needs cultivation. Fotis' wife, like all the women of her status, never had time for it.

'The idle will spread those rumours,' she said. 'They don't want to clear the land, so they expect to get rich from the stones.'

'And yet the people of the salt pans are not joking,' insisted her husband. 'They say that all the holes in the plain were dug by villagers who made their fortune looking for ancient stones.'

Yes, that's what the people of the salt pans said, and the rumours ran up and down the small settlement of Phocians. When they divided the land, they were struck by all the holes dug in the place. That is why they gradually pricked up their ears to listen to stories of buried stones. Nonetheless, over the time they had been clearing the land and preparing the soil for the plough, no one had yet dug up any sign of the treasure. Thus the matter began to slide into the realm of myth and to lose its firm grounding in the minds of the Phocians; they would have preferred a section of ploughed land, ready for sowing, to some treasure known only to God.

This ancient wall appearing before Fotis' eyes, therefore—the first sign of a world of legend—began to enliven the forgotten myth. It stirred his vivid, unruly imagination, until now unconsciously worked by so many generations of ancestors, sea-people of the Aegean.

'We should cover it,' he said to his wife, beginning to sketch out the commercial aspect of the work. 'You mustn't tell anybody anything until we see what it is. I should ask someone who knows.'

He wracked his brains.

'But who?'

'I don't know what'll come of this,' remarked the woman, maintaining her distrust. 'But I think that if you ask anyone, it should be the doctor.'

He was not of the same opinion.

'What does the doctor know about that? He's from the East too. Only people from these parts can know.'

And yet, the woman thought, led by her instinct for analogies, Dimitris too is preparing to plant a rose garden on stony ground. Why should her husband not trust him on this? They're the same…

'This is what I'll do,' said Fotis decisively. 'I'll speak to the man from Kalyvia—Green…'

The man from Kalyvia was tall, with a yellowish face, grey hair, a pointed chin and green eyes that were cold and harsh. He spoke very seldom. No one knew much about his life. He was there from the first days that the Phocians had arrived in Anavyssos. He set up a large tent and began selling bread and foodstuffs to the refugees, which he brought from the nearest village behind the hills. He did not get involved with the management of the stall, but had brought a dogsbody with him to deal with that. The green-eyed boss would sit for a little to supervise, converse with the refugees who came to buy things, and ask them about their work in the fields. He spent most of his time walking around the small plain, and the places where the Phocians were clearing. When he spoke, his words always encouraged them in their labour.

'Who could he be?' the refugees said among themselves. 'What does he want from us?'

'He wants to profit somehow. What else?'

At first they thought they could find out more about the green-eyed man from his underling, a rather clumsy villager with brown eyes, full of the cunning and feigned naivety that you find in the old Albanian villages of Attica.

They asked him, 'Your boss seems to have great wealth. What is he looking to gain here?'

The man raised his cunning eyes to the sky, covered them with a simple goodness, and replied, 'He loves the sea. That's why we came. There's no sea in Kalyvia.'

The truth is that, even if he had wanted to talk, he too knew nothing about his boss. Green had come from Lavrio to Kalyvia at the time—1911—when ancient tombs were being excavated at Anavyssos. He had worked on the excavations, but while his fellow workers saw in their labour merely an unexpected opportunity to feed themselves for a summer, Green had imagination and saw more in the soil. Rather, he saw it in the faces of the archaeologists. From their expression at each new find, he made a simple, wise estimation of its worth. He learned to read the composition of the terrain. He learned to intuit where the soil was likely to conceal ancient tombs and where not. One day they had found one of the most ancient tombs. A girl was at rest in the third stratum of earth. Her bones had become one with the soil that had covered them for thirty centuries. The villager from Lavrio went to pull one of the dead girl's hands, as if trying to help her up. The bone disintegrated in his hand, becoming earth. 'Don't!' shouted the archaeologist above. 'Don't touch it!' Then they carefully dug around the girl, until they found a lovely vase with simple figures. There was nothing fancy about it. On one side it had patterns and in its throat swelled a great, artless eye. Other vases they had found had more beautiful designs. Nonetheless, the flush over the faces of the archaeologists indicated that they considered this their best find. The villager from Lavrio thought, I could do that design myself if I tried, but I couldn't do the others. He thereby concluded he should value that which seemed possible for anyone to do. He had understood the essence of great and simple works.

Then the excavations finished, the archaeologists took the vases and left, and the girl's tomb remained open, until the rains came and turned her bones to mud and earth. The man from Lavrio was left alone, wandering around like a ghost and digging the earth of Anavyssos, until one day the rumour spread through Kalyvia that he had made a fortune. No one knew if it was gold that he had found or some other treasure.

Many girls tried to marry him. Each time he steadfastly refused. His seclusion with the ancient tombs distanced him from the living. He did not converse with anyone, his eyes became greener and his face more yellow. One or two villagers from Kalyvia had started to work for him and they gradually assimilated to the sinister personality of their master. They became silent and tricksy. They dug the earth for him. 'I don't want dawdlers,' he said. 'If you find something, you will get your money. If you don't, you won't work for me.'

That lasted some time, until the caravan of Phocians came to Anavyssos.

'We need to ask that man with the green eyes,' Fotis said to his wife. 'Only him.'

'I think he's up to no good,' she remarked.

'He's done us no harm.'

'I'm afraid of his green eyes,' she said, looking at the ground.

'Very well, but don't meddle in my decisions!'

'You know best,' she replied humbly.

The same afternoon, Fotis went to find the man. He was not at his stall. He found him on the shore, by the rocks.

'I came to ask you,' he said, 'about something only you know about.'

Green seemed to pay him no attention.

'What do you want?' he asked absent-mindedly.

'I've dug up a buried wall in my field. I think it's ancient—one of those they look for in your land.'

The green eyes swivelled around and planted themselves on him.

'Let's go!'

'Tomorrow morning,' said Fotis.

'No, now!'

'But I've covered it with earth again,' said the Phocian. 'We'll need to uncover it, and we won't have the time.'

Green did not want a second opinion.

'Yes we will!' he said, and dragged him off.

Fotis went to get his spade and pickaxe and they walked to the field. 'Ah!' he said to himself, 'He's eager. That's a good sign.'

He shovelled up the earth. The stones of the buried wall appeared under the sun that was setting over

Aegina. The green eyes inspected the wall. Potsherds were scattered in the earth. Tiles, Fotis had thought. He noticed that when Green had inspected the pit, he was excited, but took care not to show it.

'May I rent your field for three months?' he said. 'What do you want for it?'

At once, with foreboding, the Phocian understood.

'I don't want anything. It's not for rent.'

'Ten thousand,' persisted Green, his voice growing louder. 'You'll also have your field dug and you'll get it back. Do you accept?'

The amount was unsettlingly large for Fotis. He mustered all his strength to control himself.

'No,' he said. 'It's not for rent.'

Green then leapt up and seized him by his woollen clothes. He had hidden strength, and his green eyes shone.

'I'll get everything you dig up from this earth, down to the last stone!' he hissed. 'And I will pay a great price. If you aren't willing, then we'll have a reckoning!'

The Phocian took the hand that was holding him, and brought it down calmly.

'Don't be like that,' he said. 'We'll see what happens.'

Fotis returned to the settlement in a state of excitement. Aha! So is that what Green is up to? He called his wife over and told her the news, the amount he had been offered, and that he had refused.

A strange tremor came over his wife.

'Why didn't you accept?' she said. 'Why not? That's heaven sent! What are you waiting for?'

'Do you not see that for him to give such a large amount means he is expecting something extremely valuable hidden in the earth? Some old god... Why shouldn't I play him?'

'But what do we know about that?' his wife persisted. 'We will have food for the whole winter. The whole winter!'

She felt her heart beating hard. Her lips trembled with foreboding. She saw the harsh, threatening green eye fixed over them, over the peace that had begun with such effort to drip into their nights in Anavyssos.

'I'm afraid,' she whispered.

Her husband seemed to hesitate for a moment. But his stubbornness, and the idea that a door to a sudden, great fortune could be opening, stopped him definitively.

'No! We'll play all or nothing.'

CHAPTER SEVEN

Dreams of a buried god

The shacks of the Phocians gradually began to go up. The earth was sandy, but there was nothing better to be found. They made mud bricks from it. Water was a serious problem at first. They feared that the only existing well would not have enough water for them to live on, and took it sparingly. But after two or three Phocians found water and dug three more wells, the fear passed. 'It's the same vein that branches off underground,' said Matthaios, a respected elder and the only living heir to the ancient tradition of water-divining. His family had held this privilege in their homeland. It was a dark, supernatural power, which worked its will over these simple people like a dictate from above.

Indeed, the very day after they came to Anavyssos, Matthaios had looked towards the sunrise. He had a daughter-in-law and her two children with him. His son remained a prisoner in Turkey.

'Shall I hold you, Father?' said his daughter-in-law, and positioned him towards the sun.

The old man crossed himself three times, then he got onto his knees and made three prostrations, kissing the ground and praying. He stood up, took his staff and began to walk slowly, silently, fumbling along, engrossed in his task. His daughter-in-law and grandchildren followed behind. He stopped here and there, raised his staff above the earth and stood with his blind eyes fixed intently on the ground, waiting for the mystic reply of the water running dimly in the depths. Not finding it, he went on.

At last he stopped definitively.

The hand holding the staff began to tremble gently. An almost imperceptible pallor spread over that august face. It was clear how much his powers were focussed on this spot. His lips moved.

'Here,' he said, and he struck the earth with his staff.

They found the vein at a depth of twenty metres. His daughter-in-law, a stocky, unhappy young woman with a dark complexion, did most of the digging. A relative helped, but the woman took most of the burden. It was difficult work, and when she emerged from the great and ever-deepening pit, covered in sweat, she fell on the ground and broke into sobs.

'Oh, why did he have to stay?' she said, and wept for the husband she had left in Turkey. 'What will become of us? What will become of us?'

The old water-diviner stretched out his arms until he found her body, then he stroked her head.

'Dear girl,' he said, 'he'll come, you'll see. Everything will be alright.'

She got up to feed her young children. The old man stayed alone in the pit, speaking to the underground water which, moved by the hallowed staff of his ancestors, would come to light today or tomorrow, after its long and secret life.

At the foot of the small hill, next to the sea, Dr Venis' shack had now gone up. 'Shack' is not the right word. It stood out from the others because it was taller and because, having no animals, they had given greater comfort to the human spaces.

A small staircase led to a first floor, which was divided into two rooms with large windows. From there the line of Aegina was clearly visible, along with the headland of St Nicholas, Lagonisi and, further away, the line of Poros merging with that of the Peloponnese.

In the morning and evening hours, the young inhabitants of the place were accustomed to seeing from afar the feeble figure of the doctor clearing the land of lentisk and stones. Two hired Phocians did the arduous work all day long, preparing the ground. But he could not relax—as if he was unwilling to entrust to them the land that had been designated for his purpose.

From the back window, which looked onto the mountain, Irini Venis also observed the feeble shape that battled on, kneeling down and getting up again, wiping the sweat off his brow, his eyes never leaving the earth.

He was right, she thought. His ancestors follow him.

She leaned over the simple table in front of her and continued writing her letter: 'Your father is very preoccupied with his land. He is certain that next year he will have a field of roses. Then he believes that we will have every comfort from our earnings, and there will be enough to allow you to study. In the meantime, you will have to come and live with us. We have prepared your room in our shack, which is finished. You'll come, of course, with your aunt, and you'll both stay in that room. I feel terribly alone here, my dear.'

Her husband's footsteps sounded.

'The dry soil will be a great impediment to us,' he said, 'but we will struggle on.'

'I'm certain of it,' she said. After a moment she continued, 'I think my sister could now come with Anna. Then we will wait for the roses…'

He looked into her eyes.

'I think so too,' was his only reply.

She gave him the letter.

'When will the postman come?'

'Tomorrow, I suppose…' she said, before asking about her older sister. 'Do you think Maria's eyes might worsen if she comes here?'

'She has nothing to gain from being in the city. At her age she cannot have an operation, nor any more treatment.'

'It's certain, then? She can expect nothing?'

'Nothing. Gradually, she will lose her sight completely.'

The sun was setting behind Aegina. A small golden cloud was hanging over the island. Irini Venis watched it for some time, thinking about the fate of her older sister, whose adult life had certainly begun more happily than her own. Maria had loved the man who was meant for her, before disaster fell on their house. Her happiness had not lasted long, but at least she had tasted it. Her husband had died very young and she ended up, during the Great War, all alone with her young son on Aegina, where they found refuge. They spent their troubled war years there, before returning to their home, only to leave yet again. This time, however, no one came with her. Her son stayed behind.

'She could at least have one of them left…' Irini muttered.

'Why do you give up on her son?' said the doctor. 'Every so often news comes from the East. I am hopeful.'

'That's because it is in your nature. Perhaps I have lost the ability to wait.'

She folded her arms and looked out of the window.

'She is a mother and she will wait until she dies,' said Irini. Then she added, 'I think that in this the two of you are the same. You are able to wait.'

It was a gentle hour and the landscape was gentle too, and the sun was not beating on it painfully with its transformative power.

'I think you should have changed a little too, Irini,' said Dimitris softly, 'you should have got used to it... Why do you suffer so?' he asked her, and his voice was trembling.

It was one of the rare moments that her face did not have the harsh look that disarmed the weak man.

'Don't worry, Dimitris. Can one get used to things so late?'

Out of the window they saw Eleni approaching their house. The doctor pointed at her.

'Why can these simple people settle for their fate, and not us?' he said.

He felt relief when he saw Eleni. She was the help they both badly needed. Their own conversations would never end without strong words.

'Welcome!' the doctor greeted her cheerily. 'What brings you here?'

She wished them good evening and tried to smile, but it was clear she was upset and something was on her mind.

'Has something happened?' asked Dimitris.

'No, nothing,' she replied stoically. 'I came to see the lady, in case she needs some help.'

'Very well,' said the doctor, realising that she wanted to speak to his wife. 'I'll go down now.'

The two women were left alone.

'What's wrong?' asked Irini.

'Oh, m'lady, I don't know what to say!' Eleni burst out. 'But I think my husband is going against his inter-

ests and the interests of his children. I can't say anything to him. What should I do?'

Eleni made her swear that she would say nothing to
the doctor or anyone else, and then confessed the story
of the green-eyed man. She was of the opinion that
they should not refuse. With the amount he would
give them, they could build the hut they were consid-
ering for their animals and live through the winter.
What's more, she feared him. And why should they
play all or nothing? What if the god they were looking
for did not appear?

'How do you know they are looking for a god?'
asked Irini.

'No one said that, but Fotis imagines it. If it wasn't a
god, why would Green give so much?'

'And your husband knows that there are gods here?'

'Oh, everybody knows! They say the old gods of the
place are buried at the bottom of the sea and under the
ground.'

Irini Venis had also heard about the excavations
and tombs in the region of Anavyssos, but only now
did she see the legend taking shape.

'Think about it, m'lady,' insisted Eleni. 'What we
could do with all that money! If, God willing, the crops
grow, there will be nowhere for the animals. But if we
start building now, next to our shack, a roof and two
walls…'

She spoke fervently, already counting the crops and
animals that would come, and her muddled voice

strove for the most emotive note possible with which to present her vision. She found the furthest extent of her imagination, but it was still too weak to reach the gods that Fotis chased. Irini listened to her and thought about the power that moves, along with dreams, the winds and the clouds and the hearts of humans.

'I understand, Eleni,' she said, 'but you cannot do anything. You must let him decide.'

She wanted to say, 'See how my own husband is preparing a rose garden among the rocks, and I'm doing nothing about it,' but Irini Venis could not sink that low.

When the doctor returned, his wife said nothing of what Eleni had told her. She merely asked him about the man with green eyes.

'He looks suspicious,' he said, 'and I don't like him at all. He's certainly looking for something from us.'

'What do you imagine he is looking for?'

'Well…he'll be wanting to tie the villagers into debts they will have to repay threefold, or something similar.'

'You didn't hear anything else?'

'They say he's interested in antiquities. Who knows?'

CHAPTER EIGHT

The kouros of Anavyssos

Autumn came, and with it the rainy season, but above the plain and hills of Anavyssos not a cloud appeared. The earth was thirsting, and the rain would lessen the people's toil on the fallow land.

They turned to the sky, all voices pleading, 'Rain, God, rain.'

There were days when rain looked certain. The clouds thickened in the distance over Sounion, thunder rumbled and hearts started racing. The women dashed out to gather everything in, and when they had secured their belongings, the whole population went out to watch the coming rain—so much did they long for rain. They were certain of it, as if waiting for an angel to upset the water.

The black cloud came closer and closer. The earth, pine needles and sea trembled insistently—the angel was coming. Birds took flight. A few drops began to fall, sprinkling the anguished faces that were fixed on the sky.

Then something strange happened. Suddenly the cloud, as if driven off by a headwind, slightly changed its course. At that height, this tiny movement corresponded to the whole of the plain below. The cloud passed over the line of hills, shed a few drops and headed north.

The eyes of the people remained fixed on the disappearing cloud. At first they were full of surprise, but gradually that turned to despair. Silence fell over the muggy air. Then the helpless voices burst out: 'What sort of place is this! It's cursed! Even the clouds leave!'

They shouted, yelled, and the women wailed. Then someone remembered—was it the shepherds who had said this?—'The rainclouds will pass over, and not one drop will fall on the earth.'

The men seemed to be more despairing than the women, as is their nature. They give ground to imagination and disappointment. Right judgement, a weapon of self-preservation, remained the privilege of the women.

And now it was a woman who reacted to their raving. No one expected it from Irini Venis, who seemed so indifferent to the life of the shacks.

'Why are you squawking like that?' she fumed. 'Do you really believe that it never rains here and that the clouds leave? If not today, it'll rain tomorrow or the next day!'

'Yes, that's for sure!' confirmed the doctor. 'Why are we despairing? Rain will come!'

He was overjoyed with the unexpected interest shown by his wife.

'Rain will come today or tomorrow. It will!'

It will come, certainly, in the great downpours of winter. But at this time of year, when the earth is thirsting, they will see—now and next year and the next—that they will wait in vain, for the clouds will go past and leave.

'That was a great thing you did,' Dimitris Venis said to his wife that evening.

Irini, however, was shut into her icy self again. She looked at him squarely.

'If only it would never rain,' she said.

Fotis Glaros had dug all the earth in his field, but the god he was expecting was nowhere to be found. He dug deeper, at the spot where the wall was buried, but there was nothing else there, only its foundations.

Every day their shack was further rocked by the failure.

'I said so,' grumbled his wife, who had had enough. 'You didn't listen!'

And, while they looked for gods, their countrymen were every day preparing the ground so as to plant vines.

'You didn't listen!' the woman repeated bitterly.

Then Fotis reproved her so strongly that she was forced to let the matter go. But how bitter this silence was, at night when they went to sleep! The ghost of the buried god sat in between them, weighing on them. Even Fotis felt the need to speak, against his habits, to unburden himself.

'I tell you we'll find it,' he said to her with certainty. 'My heart says so.'

'Well then, let's wait for it,' she answered bitterly.

One night he startled her awake.

'Eleni! Eleni! Wake up!'

She was sleeping deeply and leapt up in surprise.

'What is it?' she cried, trying to make out some enemy in the dark.

'Shh! Don't wake the children! I saw him in my sleep! I saw him, I swear!'

He explained that he had seen the ancient god, his carved stone body taking the dusky colour of the earth in which he had rested for so many thousands of years. Fotis did not remember anything else, just the earthy colour and the closed eyelids. The god seemed to be blind.

Several days went by and the dream was forgotten. Despair had begun to grip Fotis too, when the following happened:

They had called the old water-diviner to tell them where to dig.

'At least,' Eleni had said, 'since we are digging so deep, let's see where we can find water. We'll need it when there's no rain.'

The blind water-diviner pointed to the very edge of the field.

Fotis began to dig deeper where the old man had said. His wife was a great help, going into the ever-deepening pit and shovelling earth.

One afternoon there came a flash of light. Fotis was about four metres down, and Eleni was sitting at the lip of the pit, looking at the dark, wriggling body as it dug. Oh, how strange are the workings of fate! When she left the house of the consul to marry this diminutive man, Eleni thought she knew her future. She would have children with him, suffer and, at some time if not immediately, she would come to know him—at least through the children, through the bones and the heart he passed down. Who could say with certainty, in this foreign land, above this open pit, that she had learned anything of that unknown man, anything beyond the lines of his body that crawled around down there?

A sharp, repeated note from the pit dragged her from her thoughts. The pickaxe had struck stone. She heard a groan.

'Oh no!' he cried.

She dropped onto the ground and leaned over the pit.

'What is it?' she called, frightened. 'Come up!'

'I'm hitting stone everywhere!' came the agitated voice from the pit. 'It must be bedrock!'

If you are poor and dig for a well, and God casts you onto rock, it is a true disaster. The woman knew that, but, as always, she tried to encourage him.

'Dig around it!' she shouted. 'It might not be rock.'

Then right away she added, 'I'm coming down too.'

She went down. Silently, the two of them pitted themselves against the new enemy.

The man, digging at the edge as his wife had advised, stopped for a moment.

'It's soft again here, on this side of the stone,' he said. 'What could it be?'

They bent down towards the dark earth. The woman took the spade and scraped the soil from the stone, the better to look at it. They followed its shape. It covered the length of the pit, from one side to the other, then there was a gap with earth in, and then stone again. Eleni dug out more of the earth in the gap, and above the horizontal enemy. Their nerves frayed and their hearts raced: attached to the main stone bulk appeared two hands. Then the naked body emerged in the dim light of the pit.

He grabbed her hand and squeezed it fearfully.

'That's it,' he said softly.

'Oh!' said the woman, her voice trembling, as if it were a terrible thing to raise a god.

He held her tightly by the hand and, bound together in this way as if they needed their joint powers, they sat silently above the statue, sweat pouring off their bodies.

'What now?' said Fotis.

When the fear and initial surprise had passed, he felt a deep wave of joy coursing through his body.

'What now?' he repeated, and the question had a triumphant tone. 'What should we do now?'

'What should we do?' she repeated. 'Let's cover him again and sleep on it.'

Yes, that would be best—to cover the small god and sleep on it.

Fotis had picked up the spade to start shovelling when he remembered something. He knelt over the horizontal statue and began to wipe earth from its face with his trembling hands. Sweat dripped onto the body of the god.

Finally he stopped and leaned closer. He saw. He cried, 'Look at his eyes! Look at his eyes! He's blind! Just like my dream! Like my dream!'

His wife knelt too. The two of them, more brazen by the minute, began fumbling over the stone body with its closed eyelids and hands resting against its thighs. It was a wonderful *kouros*, a monument of tenderness at rest in a stone tomb, guarded in the earth from the barbarians who had once poured over this land. The earth had kept it and given it colour, and the marble had become like earth: a material that had returned whence it came.

'How small he is!' whispered Eleni. 'Look at his fingers!'

There they stood, two insignificant beings of the world, enfolded in awe of time and the tomb, struggling to interpret the stone on which they had founded the hopes of their humble lives.

They covered the *kouros* with a thick layer of earth, waited for the sun to set and made for their shack. The cool autumn air slightly calmed their shaken nerves. They walked side by side on the path, quietly conversing, the arrival of the god separating them from the others.

'See what I said, see what I said…' Fotis was saying. 'If we had given the land, now *it* would be in someone else's hands.'

'You were right,' his wife agreed. 'You would have killed me now if you'd listened to me.'

A moment passed.

'And yet…' Eleni said.

He turned and looked at her searchingly.

'What?'

Her voice trembled a little.

'Nothing,' she replied. 'I'm just afraid. I don't know why…'

'What are you afraid of?'

She changed the subject, to avoid an explanation she could not give.

'What will you do now?' she asked him.

The question penetrated his thoughts, mingling with the flurry of joy.

'What will you do with the god now?' Eleni repeated.

How could he know? He realised that he would have to play with chance. The cunning of his seafaring ancestors, who had spent their lives dealing contraband, brought back to life the instincts that the earth had made dormant.

'We'll think. We'll play...' he said. 'Meanwhile, not a word! No one must find out anything.'

Joy was licking his limbs vigorously, watering them with strength. His small, matchstick body overflowed with a sense of health and self-sufficiency. He trod more firmly, lithely, as if subduing a hostile power. He looked down at the bare, grimy, tormented legs and silent footsteps of his wife. They were moving like independent beings sketching out their life on this soil, this earth that had created a past in his mind by sending him a message from its depths. Now a hitherto unknown tenderness was directed towards those grubby legs, and the steps that were continuing the history of the world.

In the earth, which had become mud on them, he made out a smudge of dried blood from some minor graze.

'You've cut yourself,' he said softly.

She turned to look at him, and the surprise at this new, unexpected tenderness shone in her eyes.

'What did you say?'

'Look at your leg,' he replied. 'It needs washing.'

They were nearing the village when they met the smuggler of antiquities. He was returning from the eastern hills, from his customary tour of the places they were digging. Recently he had seemed more and more het up and sullen, since nothing he hoped for had materialised, despite the Phocians' intensive digging. He had ceased going to Fotis' field when the clearing work had stopped.

He greeted them.

'Any news?'

'No, nothing.'

'The well?'

'Don't ask, boss!' Fotis said dejectedly. 'It looks like I'll be stopping for the time being.'

'Did you hit stone?'

'I hit rock and I'll need dynamite. But since the rains are coming soon, I think I'll wait for the spring.'

The green eyes fell pointedly on him.

'Quite right,' he said. 'The rains are coming.'

Zabeta, their daughter, met them in the courtyard of the shack.

'Mother, they've come!' she shouted from afar, referring to Irini Venis' sister and daughter. 'The lady has come with the girl! They were looking for you at the doctor's house!'

Eleni lit the oil lamp, put water to boil for their evening meal, hastily saw to her children and then made for the house of Dimitris Venis.

Aunt Maria was much older than Irini. Her white head of hair cast a gentle light on her weak, pale face and its fading eyes. On her face remained the marks of a nobility that would not disappear even beneath the layers of disaster.

She was sitting near the window, and the small circle of lamplight was extending the kindness of her face onto the surrounding people. Next to her sat her younger sister, Irini, and then the doctor. Standing up, glowing in the youth of her sixteen years, her dark hair flowing, was the Venises' daughter, Anna.

Eleni approached the old noblewoman bashfully, bending down to kiss her hand.

'Welcome, my good lady. We were expecting you.'

The eyelashes on the aged face of the older sister fluttered, as if trying to focus her memory.

'Thank you, my dear,' she said softly. But, frustrated in her attempt to remember, she asked, 'Who are you?'

'Eleni, Fotis Glaros' wife.'

'Oh, it's you! How are you all?'

She thanked her, saying that everyone was well. Very well indeed. She wished, flooded as she was with the emotion of the little god—their saving grace— that she could shout for joy and tell all these beloved people about it. But she remembered her husband and restrained herself.

She greeted Anna and then went down to take care of the fire and dinner for the Venises. When she returned to her own shack, exhausted, she gave the news to her husband.

'The poor lady seems to be losing her sight. She didn't recognise me.'

'Everyone has their troubles,' Fotis mused, before asking, 'Is she still waiting for her son to return?'

'Who isn't waiting for their loved ones? I am certain that Christ will keep them safe.'

She prepared food for her children and her husband; she was not hungry.

'It must be from joy,' said Fotis.

She did not know what to say.

'Yes, it must be.'

'If all goes to plan, you won't have to tire yourself out at the doctor's house,' said Fotis. 'We'll have enough to pay him when need be.'

'But I don't mind helping them. They're good people.'

She extinguished the lamp and they lay down together, the peace of the desolate place covering their bodies.

Lying in the darkness, Eleni could not close her eyes. There was a strange agitation, an unrest in her heart, a tightening in her throat… and in the pitch darkness hovered the small, lean body of the god that had come to light, with its closed eyes, its hands resting against its thighs, its sallow colour.

She sensed that her husband beside her, blanket pulled up to his chin, was also lying awake. His breath was rapid and tremulous, she noticed, different from the deep and serene breath of repose. She said nothing, however, in case sleep was coming gradually. Outside the door of the shack she felt the gentle trembling of the night merging with the sound of the ocean—a dark and pitiless confirmation of eternity.

Many hours went by. Sleep did not come.

Fotis was first to rise.

'Do you want anything?' she asked him at once, softly.

'Oh, you're awake too?' he said. 'It's hot. I'm going out.'

'Where are you going?' she asked, concerned. 'It's still night.'

'It doesn't matter. I'll go to the field.'

She felt an indefinable danger, which she was reluctant to admit—a danger circling around the deep tomb.

He dressed and went out. The coolness of dawn enfolded him and lent a briskness to his blood. The morning star had risen over the hills. Dewy light was dripping.

He was close to his field when he thought he heard footsteps in the darkness. His heart beat harder. He quickened his step. The voiceless body appeared.

It was Green, returning from the direction of Fotis' field. When Fotis saw him, he was gripped by a sinister foreboding. He felt an indeterminate sense of fear and hatred.

They halted, face to face with one another.

'Where are you going at this hour?' asked Green.

Fotis replied that he always starts work at dawn. He couldn't sleep.

'But,' he asked, 'where are *you* going?'

'Nowhere,' Green muttered through clenched teeth. Then he shrugged and headed for the sea.

Fotis reached the field and stopped above the open pit. He looked into the dark depths, where his fate lay, then sat on the pile of earth they had dug up. He looked at the sky, far out over the open sea, and dew soaked his body. How fine it is to exist, with the certainty of a strong body that reacts and trembles, and with your own earth beneath your feet! Now, he thought, everything will change. Two grubby legs follow him, exhausted, over the land. The small surrounding hills have disappeared; borders have vanished. Now the whole world belongs to him. And the two tormented legs keep walking, and are suddenly covered with blood. 'Watch your legs,' he says to her. 'They'll hurt.'

He jumped up, pierced by the cold. The morning star had disappeared. The lines of the Anavyssos hills began to appear in the low light of dawn.

He walked a little, to come round from his numbness. When daylight came he descended into the pit.

It immediately looked strange. There were piles of earth on one side. And yet yesterday evening they had pitched all the earth over the statue. Fear penetrated his body. At once he dropped to the ground and began scrabbling wildly with his hands in the dirt, feeling for the statue. What was he looking for here? What was he looking for? His mind went back and forth to Green, but he did not dare to draw a conclusion.

At last his fingers, bleeding and hurting, touched marble.

He breathed a sigh of relief.

'Thank God!'

He wiped his hands on his clothes and then wiped the sweat off his brow.

I must make a decision, he thought. I should approach him today and see what he thinks it is. Most importantly though, someone needs to stand guard.

CHAPTER NINE

The flood

Nothing about the dawn of that day presaged its end. Just a few clouds were travelling towards the south. The sun was sure to disperse them.

'Listen!' said Fotis to his wife, when she came to the field to find him. 'You must not leave here until I return! I'll come in the early evening. Now I'm going to Thymari.'

Since he had nothing to do at the well, he decided to go to the other field behind the headland. He would come back early and look for Green. He would talk to Green obliquely, primarily so he would not think that he was in a rush. Then he would come to sleep above the pit, until he had dealt with the matter.

'Got it? You must not move from here!' he told her again.

He paused.

'I saw him wandering around here this morning, you see,' he added.

She did not ask who; she understood.

Her secret fears awakened again. She was about to say, 'What will you do at Thymari? Why today? Go and find him, make an agreement and bring this to an end.' But she said nothing.

'Very well. I will stand guard here until you return.'

She watched him go off jauntily.

'Give some bread to the children,' she shouted from afar. 'Tell them not to wait for me.'

How did the sky suddenly fill with so many clouds?

The black beasts sprung up from behind the line of hills that cut off the horizon, rising one after the other as if stirred from the bowels of the earth. There are no trees here on the plain to rustle their leaves and warn of the storm. There is no lightning, no thunder, just a mute, dark, deathlike mass. How different everything was on the eastern shores! There the rain, the cold and the warm days all came at their appointed time, sending first one message, then another. Nothing was abrupt and violent, and the people were able to prepare themselves, the body gathering strength to resist.

Eleni sat all alone in the foreign land and felt the dark mass of the sky gradually encircling her. She felt more and more vulnerable and alone above the open pit.

'May God protect us all!'

Then, suddenly, the heavens opened with phenomenal, terrifying force. There was no wind, so the rain fell vertically, and shockingly hard.

The earth drank, drank, drank. Then, unable to take more water, it began to drive it to the sea. Everywhere the ditches filled, becoming little rivers running downwards.

An hour went by, then another and another. The terror showed no sign of abating. Eleni had sheltered in the ruins of the chapel, and was praying constantly.

'My God, so much water… It's too much. We did not want so much…'

Her eyes, staring through the muggy air at the dense waves of the downpour, gradually became weary, and her strength to withstand it began to fade. How fine it would be if everything were so futile that people would not even *try* to do anything! And so they would sit plunged in certainty, their limbs at rest, feeling no pain. How many times in her life had she really lived, or been at ease to see the world around her? A flower, a man, a star, a horse… Many things seemed beautiful in this world, but how could she know? She and all others of her position only knew what was useful. The value of everything was measured against this standard: the cloud that rained at its appointed time, the cloudless night that dispelled fear, the green earth that gave this year's crop and next year's seed. The pine is a good tree for it gives resin and firewood. She is bound to things by instinct, which surpasses sensibility. But that is to abandon their beauty, for beauty begins where necessity ends.

How many hours went by? The rain started to lighten. The change stirred the dozing body of the poor woman into action. She shook out her hands a couple of times.

What time is it? she thought.

Then she wondered what had happened to her children down in the shacks. Would Zabeta have managed to gather everything inside? And her husband at Thymari? Where had he sheltered? Eleni's care for everyone—her only purpose in life—took hold again as soon as her faculties awoke from their torpor.

The rain was falling lightly now. She decided to leave the chapel to stretch her legs. Around her she heard a low rumble from the streams where the dirty water ran.

She kept walking. Then, suddenly, she noticed it.

Over the rumble of the streams was another deep, muffled din coming from the area of their shacks.

Is it the sea? she asked herself.

No, it wasn't waves. If it was, it would be coming and going.

Now this muffled thing came from high up.

What is it? she wondered.

Within the rumble of water, she thought she could make out human voices.

She listened closely. Something like a deep, submerged lowing was coming from the shacks.

She went a step closer, then another, more agitated. She broke into a run. The sinister rumbling became clearer as she went on. It's a river, she suddenly thought, and wondered how she had not thought of this sooner. How had this happened? And where was the river running?

People's voices became more distinct in the rumble of water.

Has the water reached the village?

A mass of mad fantasies began to play out before her eyes. She saw her children, alone and defenceless, struggling against the watery fiend; she heard their helpless voices among the voices of the crowd.

'My God!' she said, and ran faster and faster. 'God, protect us!'

She was soaked through and her bare legs sank to their knees in mud.

'Protect us!' she begged.

Soon she arrived at the wall of water.

It was a broad river, hurtling down from the hills. The deep, sandy footpath, which went to the fields, had become a fast-flowing river. How had they not suspected this? This deep path went through their shacks to the sea.

'Oh, dear God!' said Eleni. 'The shack will be flooded…'

She could not see through the haze to the opposite bank. The voices became clearer and clearer, insistent and desperate.

It can't be deep, she thought.

Driven by the cries, she crossed herself and waded into the river.

She went gingerly, step by step. Fear danced in her eyes. There was nothing else to do. 'Help us, God!' she cried. Another step. Then suddenly one of her feet trod into emptiness. She plunged into the river, stepping with the other foot to find a grip and get out of the hole. The cloudy water crashed onwards, dragging wood and tree trunks with it. She realised there was nothing beneath her feet. She stretched out her hands, but it was useless.

Now the water carried down a body, along with the wood.

There's a lot of water. But it's a strange place. For so much rain to fall, it should mean that the ground is used to taking it, Fotis thought. He was sitting under a juniper tree in Thymari looking at the rain, which was now weakening. The water did not remind him of death as much as the earth did. When he was a child he had seen a drowned man. It was a goatherd who had been grazing his goats on some rocks on the coast. The goatherd fell from high and the sea dragged him down and held him on its bed, as he cleaved to a rock down there. The goats grazed for many hours above, but he remained unmoving on the seabed. When the others had scoured the place and found him, no one wanted to go into the sea to detach the body, for they all feared the wrath of the water. The women sat above on the rocks and made their laments. It was dead calm then, so the people above on the rocks could see the seaweed waving next to the drowned man on the seabed. The fish were brazen, going into his nostrils and up to his open eyes, coming to terms with him. It was as if the body was starting a new life underwater—with nothing of the deathliness of the earth, where worms lie in wait in the darkness.

'Oh, how sweet water is!' Fotis said to himself; that was all that surfaced in his mind after his deep journey. 'And the worms in the earth will wait for the water on rainy days, with their blind eyes fixed upwards and their mouths open. Oh, how it will taste in their waiting mouths…'

He felt a powerful joy swelling in his chest. The worms with their blind eyes. With their blind eyes!

The word 'blind' suddenly brought him back to the previous night.

What will the rain have done? he wondered, thinking about the small, blind *kouros*. It will be floating in the pit… but tonight I will find Green. We'll come to an arrangement. And it will all be over.

He emerged from his hideout and walked resolutely back towards the shacks. It was now only drizzling.

She'll have sheltered in the chapel, he thought, his mind turning to his wife. She won't have moved from there.

Did she get wet? Possibly. Her face and legs would have got wet. Then, beside the image of her sodden body, he remembered the smudge of blood on her legs yesterday.

Now she'll be able to rest…since we found the god…

This unexpected tenderness was a new sensation. When you are poor and troubled, there is no time for pity—such things need stillness. First, the body was made with clay, and much later the heart was put inside—perhaps on the day the stars were made.

Now she'll be able to rest…

He walked on, calm and relaxed. Behind the clouds, the sun must be heading towards its setting place. The sea was rough beside him. He whistled a tune from his homeland.

He had turned the headland and was nearing their dwellings when he met another villager.

'Where are you going?' he cried. 'At the shacks there's complete havoc!'

'What's happened?'

He told Fotis swiftly. The river has flooded the village. The mud bricks are becoming mush. A dozen shacks have been destroyed. The place is a lake.

'Is my wife there?' asked Fotis desperately.

He did not know. But he thought she was. In any case, no one was hurt. He wanted to say: 'There are no casualties.'

Fotis arrived at the village, breathless.

The women's voices were consonant with the turbulent sky and ocean. A rhythmic clanging mingled with the roar of the sea: a petrol-powered caïque was rounding the headland, making for Sounion.

Fotis' shack had held up, but the river had been flooding for many hours and it was still floating like a boat. They told him that his children had been given shelter with the doctor.

'Where have you been in all this chaos? Where is your wife?' asked Dimitris Venis.

Fotis looked at him desperately. His lips and his whole body were shaking.

'Where is my wife? You mean she hasn't appeared all day?'

It was a pointless thing to say, for he knew she would not have left her post. 'Wait for me here!' he said. He knew that whatever happened she was not to leave the open pit.

He went at a run towards the field of the little god. He had to climb up high to find a shallow place to cross the river. Not a soul could be heard. The earth was mute as the falling night. Only the water filling the scattered holes and the streams made strange sounds.

'Eleni!'

He took a deep breath, quashed the fear rising from the depths of his body and shouted again: 'Eleni! Where are you?'

He searched in the chapel, went to the pit, looked everywhere while shouting her name. No response came. Not even the earth echoed back. Only the sound of the water.

Fear, slimy and lizard-green, glistened over his body. He ran back to the village. He was suddenly aware of the preciousness of that sweet, suffering face, which he now sought so desperately.

'My wife's disappeared! My wife's disappeared!' he cried to the villagers, and ran to the doctor's house, looking for support.

Everyone was thrown into a panic. His children, not fully understanding what was happening, started wailing. In the flooded village, the incident overshadowed all the other complaints.

'Let's go out with lanterns and look,' said the doctor, pale and shaken, to the people who had gathered at his house. 'Don't panic!'

'Where are you going?' cried Irini, exasperated at the commotion. 'For God's sake, will no one calm down here!'

The doctor now looked so piercingly at her that she withdrew.

'Shame...' he said quietly.

They took the lanterns and lit torches, and the small search-party scattered in the night along the length of the river.

The children found this unexpected procession strange. It was a change to the monotonous village life. They ran screeching behind the adults.

Dimitris Venis hurried along with them, leaning on the arm of his daughter.

'Anna, you did not have to come,' he said. 'You'll get wet.'

'No, I didn't have to come,' she replied simply.

Walking next to him, he knew the young body was moved by the misery of the world. He squeezed the arm that supported him.

'How did this happen? How?' Dimitris said. 'How were we so blind not to see that the path was a river—?'

He paused. Above the other voices of the procession shouting for the lost woman, above the noise of the water, came a frenzied voice, fearfully tearing the night.

'Here!' the desperate voice shouted. 'Come here!'

The lit torches and lanterns turned at once and came running towards the voice, as if driven by the four winds.

The voice was calling from the border of a field, whose owner had surrounded it with wire fencing as it was close to the village. The river ran along its boundary. There the drowned body was dangling on the surface of the murky river, skirt and long hair entangled in the wire. The water, its path obstructed, lapped around the legs, the throat.

She was laid on the ground floor of the doctor's house. Anna supervised while the Phocians washed the body, combed the hair and cleaned off the mud and earth of the hills. They stuck a small candle onto a copper plate. The dead woman's children wept over her for a short while, before being taken away. The village women remained alone with her, keening.

Irini Venis came down briefly, saw the body and

was so shaken that she had to be helped up to her room. She was livid.

'Why didn't you take her elsewhere? Why not? And *you*, how can you stand this horror?' she cried at her daughter, who was trying to console her.

'But they are so miserable!' she responded, holding back her indignation. 'And that woman worked so faithfully for us!'

'Well, I'm miserable too! I can't take this anymore!'

Anna put her to bed and went downstairs. She glanced around for her father, and saw him sitting next to Aunt Maria, near the dead woman, along with the other peasants. His arms were folded and his face was the colour of death—the same colour as the face of the dead woman.

'Poor Father...' she said affectionately.

Fotis was sitting in a corner, looking at the candle and the lifeless face. She is at peace now, but what has she left behind? Why, why did this evil have to arrive just when the good days were beginning?

Only now did his mind start to focus on one single point. The lifeless, motionless face merged with something else, becoming pale, buried stone... What has happened in the pit?

Fear gripped him whole. The joints of life again became stronger than anything, even death.

He leapt up.

'I'll be gone briefly, very briefly,' he said, agitated, to the others staying up with his wife.

The night was thick. He splashed through the water, running to his field. He looked for the shallow place to cross the river. In any case, the water was lower now.

Finally he arrived at the open pit. He went down cautiously, fumbling blindly. His heart beat hard. He fell on the ground and began to turn over the earth with his hands. It had become mud.

His fingers found the place. He groped wildly in the earth. But he already knew it was futile.

The little god was not there.

When he returned to his dead wife, covered in mud and with bloodied fingers, the others were puzzled: 'Where were you all this time?'

'I was looking for Green,' he said with a madman's voice. 'Don't suppose you've seen him?'

How could they have seen him? He had carried it off so well! He had ordered his minions to cut the *kouros* in two, as it was too heavy to lift. Then they had put the two pieces in sacks and carried them to the sea, as if the *kouros* were any old cargo.

'Don't suppose you've seen him?' Fotis repeated, desperately.

'I saw him!' one replied. 'He's raving mad. He set off in his petrol boat, in this weather! He was heading south.'

Fotis began to wail, before the drowned body, more bitterly than he had for the dead woman.

'I'm done for now! I'm done for!' he wailed.

He beat his chest, saying incoherent things about a god that was stolen from him.

'He's lost it,' said the others compassionately, and took him away from the body.

The same night, the Arvanites were waiting in their huts for the man they had sent down to see what had happened in Anavyssos following the downpour.

'Well?' asked the elder, as soon as he arrived.

'Just as you said. The water went right through their shacks and wiped out most of them. They're in despair.'

'Let's see, then, who will survive—them or us!' said the elder.

Then, turning to the others: 'Not a word! No one must find out what happened with the streams! Otherwise we'll be in trouble.'

They all agreed not to say a word about what had happened a few nights earlier when they blocked off the ditches that dispersed water at the bottom of the hill, making it pour from all sides into the broad path that went among the shacks of Anavyssos.

As for Eleni, they buried her the next day beside the ruined chapel, in their field, next to the old tomb. Thus she would be close to their hopes and dreams. The earth is the surest, the strongest. It will guard this body too, until another generation comes, and then another, and nothing will remain in memory of its passing. Then will come the final repose.

'Dust thou art, and unto dust shalt thou return,' said the doctor softly. He was doing the priest's duties. The death reminded them of that great lack.

'We will need to find a priest. We are Christians after all,' said one of them.

'And choose a place for the cemetery,' said another.

'Behind Thymari there is a sheltered place you cannot see from anywhere. There!' said a third.

'No, we shall make it on the small hill, opposite our shacks,' said the others. 'We will not separate ourselves from our dead!'

All of them thus agreed to make their cemetery there, among their shacks, on the pine-clad hill. For they had the familiarity with death that simple people have: those who are bound to the earth and things of the world.

CHAPTER TEN

Aunt Maria

At the foot of Olympus, the most distant mountain in the area, another group of refugees came to settle. They were from the Anatolian mainland.

They built their shacks such that no window looked out to sea, down towards Anavyssos.

The Phocians met these Anatolians now and then on the footpaths of the villages, or they saw them from afar, climbing over the craggy hills, digging non-stop. The cleared area now extended in ever-higher terraces up the mountain. It was a work of patience and instinct, undermining the composure of the mountain.

'What strength they have!' the Phocians said to themselves, observing their struggle.

Though they also struggled, at least it was with a plain. What could the others expect from the rocks?

They said as much, but the others shook their heads patiently.

'God looks after us, too…'

'You could go further down,' the Phocians said. 'Beyond the salt pans there is so much fallow land!'

They did not want to admit it, but occasionally one would let slip the real reason.

'It's that devil!' they would say, pointing at the sea.

'But what will the sea do to you?' asked the Phocians in bewilderment. 'See how we built our shacks next to it.'

'Yes, but you're different.'

For them, this endless water was a strange and hostile beast. Most of them had seen the sea only with the exchange of populations, when they were carried off from their lands to the coast and put on boats to Greece.

Their fathers and forefathers only knew the land, and beyond the mountains more land, without end. The earth followed them like the blood in their veins. They did not know the meaning of rest. They worked and dug, with an animal's instinct to find refuge. They knew that the earth they were clearing would give them food and seed—and, later, a tomb.

Very rarely, on a festival day and with the weather fine, they would go down to the sea for a walk. Large groups of families sat on the beach and looked at the sea with expressionless eyes. The most interesting thing to them was not the waves. It was the white pyramids and the great pans that held the water until it dried and became salt. It seemed to them a great work of the devil, this tamed water. They did not like to go to the Phocians' village much. From the sand where they were sitting they heard their songs and shook their heads deploringly: 'How idle and stupid they are!'

It was not easy for them to understand the nature of the people from the coast. It seemed particularly incomprehensible that so many Phocian families had left people in the East. How, then, could they have forgotten them and be making merry?

The rains now came regularly, but in patches, never lasting the whole day.

On those days the Phocians would sit in their huts and relax, for they knew that the water was preparing the earth, fertilising the roots of the vines that would grow when the time came.

Fotis, however, could not stand this stagnancy. In his small body his nerves became tangled with his veins like a ship's rigging. In the first days after the misfortune took his wife and the small, blind *kouros*, he had fallen into great melancholy. Many said that he would not lift his head high again. At Doctor Venis' house, when they talked about him, Anna was of the same opinion. She went to Fotis' shack and saw to the family regularly, helping Zabeta, the little girl, who had now taken on the care of the two other small children by herself.

'He is completely desperate,' Anna told her father. 'He won't improve.'

The doctor, however, understood people better and disagreed.

'He will. You'll see,' he said. 'He's a sturdy fellow. We won't let him go.'

He took him to the wasteland intended for the roses and started digging to set an example.

'Soon we'll plant the canes,' he said. 'Then we'll wait for the roses.'

Fotis stood silently and looked at the stony, barren ground and the sea, so hostile to the other race.

'What do you say now?' Dimitris continued. 'Will the roses grow or not?'

He hesitated, unsure what to reply. The opinion of all the villagers was that the doctor was foolishly wasting his effort. They tried to win him over, but it was useless. They were sure it was hopeless, but at heart they were envious of his faith, for they came from the same race and within them stirred the same passion for wild acts of the imagination.

'You will see a new species of rose growing, sprinkled with salt!' they joked.

Since then they had called the place, and the wild mountain above it, the 'rose garden'. It was a means of orientation, but at heart it was the voice that told them to believe.

'Well?' said the doctor to Fotis. 'Will the roses grow or not?'

Bowing to the fire of belief, he responded, 'They'll grow.'

Then Dimitris laid aside the pickaxe, sat on the ground and tried to breathe strength into him.

'Don't get yourself down with the same old things,' he said. 'What happened to us in the East has happened only a few times in the history of the world. But we have started again from scratch. Don't think any more about the stone you lost. It was no god.'

Fotis had told him the whole story of the ancient tomb. And Dimitris said that the wife he lost was much more valuable than the carved stone. It is the destiny of us all to leave. He, a strong man, must not let himself be carried off just because death came to his house.

'I should get onto him,' Fotis said about Green. 'The authorities would be on my side.'

The doctor told him that the law was no use, since he had trespassed on and concealed an ancient statue that belonged to the nation.

One day, Fotis said to Dimitris Venis, 'I see land beyond the sea. If I had a way of travelling, I would make ends meet. There's nothing to be done with the earth.'

Dimitris, who understood the hearts of men, saw in that desire the awakening of life.

'Yes, that's right!' he encouraged him. 'In these waters a felucca would be enough. Try it!'

Fotis went as a deckhand on a couple of trips to Aegina and Poros with the caïque from the salt pans. They brought back sacks of grain. He took a little of the profit and saved it. On the next trip he added to his savings. And on the next.

In the salt pans there was a small dockyard. Fotis gathered all his savings from his trips, and the state subsidies, took out a small loan, and put it all in the dockyard. Soon his vessel was launched—a fishing boat freshly painted with bright colours and two ribbons: one yellow, one red.

'Now we'll wait for the weather to ease,' said Fotis, 'and then she'll earn us some bread.'

He delighted in his vessel, and in the letters of its name printed on the bow: *Eleni*.

With the rains, Aunt Maria was having trouble getting out. The Phocians now saw the devoted couple less often—Aunt Maria with Anna Venis, walking slowly along the coast path to Thymari. The old woman would lean on the arm of the girl, who was much taller than her, and their silhouettes appeared in the blue distance as if they were walking towards their destiny.

Irini Venis never wanted to accompany them. She would refuse in her icy voice, and they knew that to persist would be in vain.

There was little conversation between the two walkers on the road, as the old woman tired easily and because there were many things between them that could not come to the surface.

They always walked to the same point—up to the second headland.

'Here we are again,' Aunt Maria said every time, as if needing to confirm the event.

Then they would sit on a lonely rock above the sea. Centuries of storms and waves have battered it, and small holes have been hollowed out. When the storm recedes, a little water is left in the holes before the sun dries it. The salt remains, and the fishermen, who come occasionally in their boats to shelter there, gather it for their soup. On the leeward parts of the coast, you can find smoke-blackened hollows in the rock where they have lit fires in their brief passage through.

The silent, graceful lines of Aegina are visible in the distance.

'How many miles do you think it is from here?' asked the girl absent-mindedly about the island of her childhood.

'How many miles? Who knows?'

A boat was passing, heading for the islands. They faintly heard the deep rumble of its engines.

'Last night I counted all the passing boats with lights on,' said Anna. 'There were thirty…'

'Did you stay up so late again?'

'I couldn't sleep.'

'How did I not notice, my dear? I would not have left you.'

Then she added, 'If only we could also see the incoming boats….'

The boats always came in at dawn, heading to Piraeus from all corners of the world. One day, one of them would bring her child who had remained in the East, Angelos. It would pass here and she would be asleep and know nothing.

'Do you think he will find out easily that we are here?'

She need not worry, the girl assured her. All their compatriots in Piraeus knew that the Phocians were in Anavyssos.

'They'll come together, of course, as when they left,' Anna remarked.

'Angelos, you mean?'

'Yes, and Andreas.'

The old woman stroked the girl's hand.

'Yes, my dear. They will come together.'

Anna had said nothing to her, but she could guess the girl's thoughts from the slight wobble in her voice—a secret message, and God's smile.

'Yes, my dear. They will come together.'

The sea merged with their anticipation, with their expectant voices, and it too became an element of life —the waves that would carry their dreams.

CHAPTER ELEVEN

*Captain Scott, the South Pole, Dimitris Venis
and the Saronic Gulf*

'There, Sophia,' said Aunt Maria to the old woman at her side, Andreas' mother. 'There's a bookmark on the page...'

'Yes, here, I've found it,' she replied.

She began to read from the Scriptures in the waning evening light:

'And the damsel was very fair to look upon, a virgin, neither had any man known her: and she went down to the well, and filled her pitcher, and came up. And the servant ran to meet her, and said, "Let me, I pray thee, drink a little water of thy pitcher." And she said, "Drink, my lord": and she hasted, and let down her pitcher upon her hand, and gave him drink. And when she had done giving him drink, she said, "I will draw water for thy camels also, until they have done drinking." And she hasted, and emptied her pitcher into the trough, and ran again unto the well to draw water, and drew for all his camels.'[6]

The two mothers then fell into the deep peace given by the strength of the moving sea, the motionless sky, the poetry of humankind. They remained silent for a long while.

'They will have grown up a lot in the time that's passed, those two,' said one of the mothers. 'Do you think his suit will fit him when he comes back?'

'So you too took one of his suits when we left?'

'Why, did you, Maria?'

'I did, Sophia.'

'It doesn't matter if they're too small now. Let's just hope they come.'

'Yesterday, Anna was remembering their childhood on Aegina,' Aunt Maria said to Andreas' mother after a while. 'They lived so much together, you see—Angelos, Andreas and her…'

'Yes, they did.'

'Anna is awaiting their return as much as we are,' said Aunt Maria. 'Do you realise that?'

'I do,' said Andreas' mother tenderly.

Everyone was gathered around Dimitris Venis—Aunt Maria, Irini and Anna. Andreas' mother, Aunt Sophia,

---

[6] *Genesis* 24:16

was now visiting their house regularly. She and Aunt Maria understood each other. Both were waiting for their children to return from imprisonment.

Irini Venis very rarely took part in the group's conversations. Day by day she was becoming sourer and more on edge.

'What is it?' her sister asked. 'You're becoming miserable. Look at me,' she said, fixing her clear, serene face on her, 'I am all alone, and I can survive just on hope.'

'Not on hope alone,' she responded bitterly. 'On the past too. Whereas I—'

'That is no one's fault, Irini. It was the will of God. But it does not seem such a terrible punishment for you to get this good man. At least he is alive.'

'And what about me?' said Irini.

. . . .

Dimitris was cleaning his glasses. The book before him was open invitingly, and the group around him waited, expectant. He liked to imagine that all of them were anxious to listen, and the thought made him happy as a child.

'Will it be about Napoleon?' asked Irini coldly.

'No. It will be from the diary of Captain Scott.'

'Very well. Then it will be about Napoleon tomorrow.'

That was his luggage when he set out for Anavyssos: a history of Napoleon Bonaparte, a biography of Captain Scott and a textbook on pathology.

Dimitris began to read slowly. His eyes lit up and a light pink colour flooded his pale face as he turned the pages of passion set in the tragic silence of the ice.[7]

'How much endless time do the shadows need to encircle us…they proceed slowly on our right, only to disappear on our left with the swift darkness,' Scott notes.

Later: 'Only 90 miles to the Pole. But if things continue like this, we cannot endure it.'

'Still 85 miles to the Pole, but we'll spit blood.'

'Only 60 miles left, and if we do not reach the end, we will have been unimaginably close.'

'Still 40 miles and the end is in our grasp.'

'Still 30 wretched miles. We must reach it, whatever the cost.'

'16th January 1912. High spirits.'

There are only five people in the fearful white wasteland and they are heading for the simple point where they know that no human voice has been heard since the moment earth was made a solid mass. They are the first. 'High spirits.' Then, at that great moment, one of the companions, Bowers, appears uneasy. His eye seems to be fixed on a dark point in the endless wilderness. He does not dare say anything to the others. But the others see it and are gripped

---

[7] The following is taken from the writings of Stefan Zweig—*Triumph and Disaster: five historical miniatures*—and the diaries of Captain Scott.

with terror at the thought that a human hand has set up a sign there. Could it be a crevice in the ice, or a reflection? They continue with frayed nerves, trying to deceive themselves, even though they all know the truth: Amundsen and the Norwegians have overtaken them. The final doubt, however, flees in the face of the bitter reality: a black flag waving on a pole and the signs of a makeshift human encampment. This colossal, inconceivable event, that the South Pole, soulless for thousands of years, was discovered twice within two weeks. And they were second. They were too late. They were second—and for humanity, first is everything and second nothing. 'All our effort, all our trials, all our suffering... For what?' writes Scott in his diary. 'For nothing... All the daydreams must go.'

Despondent, like convicts, they begin the last march on the Pole. They do not try to console one another. On the 18th of January, Captain Scott and his companions arrive at the Pole. They look sadly at the solemn place. 'No one can see anything here, nothing that is different from the awful monotony of the past days.' That is all.

They begin the return journey.

'I fear the return,' writes Scott in his diary. Without hope, without the help of a compass, they fear that they will lose their tracks and the equipment that they left on the way. Going off course means death. The weather becomes more and more hostile. Winter begins earlier than other years. The cold wears down their exhausted, blistered bodies. Evans, the strongest of all of them, suddenly starts acting strangely. They know he has gone mad. What can they do with him? Abandon him in the wilderness? The wind blows stronger than ever. 'God help us. We were not meant for these exertions.' 'Our game is ending tragically. Let Divine Providence help us now, we cannot expect any other help.' They drag themselves through the ice. They begin to prepare themselves. They ask to share the morphine, for their final hour. One, Oates, can only just follow. He staggers to the night camp. He sleeps with them until the morning. The blizzard is raging. Oates gets up. 'I am just going outside,' he says to his companions, 'and may be some time.'

The others tremble, knowing what this walk means. But no one dares to stop him. They all understand and respect that their friend Lawrence Oates will walk to his death a hero.

The three of them that are left continue. Their oil is finished and the thermometer shows -40°C. Their provisions have run out. On the 29th of March they know that not even a miracle can save them. They decide not to take even one step towards fate, but nestle into their sleeping bags. And of their final suffering not the smallest groan was heard on earth.

Months later, after a rescue party had been organised, their bodies were found frozen in their sleeping bags, as if they were asleep. They found Scott embracing Wilson fraternally in death. A farewell letter, written by his frozen hands to his best friend in England, read, 'I never met a man in my life whom I admired and loved more than you, but I never could show you how much your friendship meant to me, for you had much to give and I nothing.'

That letter of a man who 'had nothing to give' was signed by Captain Scott.

· ·

He finished. He was pale and his fingers were trembling. He closed the book slowly.

The two mothers of the missing boys did not stir, but were rooted there with emotion. Irini rose ostentatiously and went out.

'How many times have I heard that...'

Anna, sitting next to her father, was shaken. She got up and kissed him on the forehead.

There were days when the west wind blew with fearful might over the entire Saronic Gulf, rousing great waves. The terror that raged out at sea arrived much depleted in Anavyssos, dying down in the mouth of the small bay. But the sea became inky black and trembled from the squalls that whipped nimbly across it.

Aunt Maria was sitting at the window and, as she could not see far, Anna was trying to enlighten her on the happenings outside.

'Can you see waves outside the bay?' asked Aunt Maria.

'I can see still white mountains.'

'Then we'll certainly be seeing masts tomorrow morning at St Nicholas.'

This happened every time there was a strong wind. Ships coming or going from Piraeus and unable to fight the storm would drift into the calm embrace of St Nicholas under jib alone. They would drop anchor there, waiting for the weather to subside before they set sail again. Most often, ships that happened upon these waters at night found refuge there.

In the morning the inhabitants of Anavyssos would see a small sea of masts—a sign of God's victory over men.

'We are sure to see them again tomorrow morning,' Aunt Maria said to Anna.

She said 'we will see them', but she meant 'you will see them and you will tell me.' She was now used to seeing the world through those other eyes that she had taught to see for her.

'Are they there?' she asked Anna early next morning, as if she needed her expectations confirmed.

'They are.'

'Are there many?'

'Oh, it's a forest! There! There!'

With her hands, the girl tried to guide the line of sight of the half-blind woman towards the forest.

'There, there!'

The fading eyes opened wide, trying to focus their powers towards the distant sight. They remained there, fixed in their effort, like solitary beings just starting life.

'Can you see, Aunt Maria?'

'Yes, yes, I can. There are many.'

Then she relaxed in the illusion of the miracle. And, her goal accomplished, she said, 'May God give them fine weather soon, so they can leave.'

At St Nicholas, where the troubled ships were lying, there is a tongue of land that is one of the most serene places in the area. A narrow strip of sand links the northern hills of Anavyssos, steep over the shore to St Nicholas. Beyond the strip there is another small bay, which tames the waves as they come from the open sea of the gulf. It tames the wind as well, so that it arrives in the bay of St Nicholas without any force. Hence St Nicholas, in its privileged spot at the mouth of the bay of Anavyssos, is the most blessed refuge in a storm. Next to the chapel there is a deep well. Thus the ships' crews, barring rare circumstances, have no need to take the hour's path that leads through the hills to the village of Anavyssos.

The inhabitants of the shacks see the forest of masts as a game that disturbs the monotony of their days, and when they get up in the morning and do not see the masts in place, it is as if some enchantment came and disappeared without touching them.

'The wind has fallen,' Aunt Maria murmured, waking up suddenly in the middle of the night and talking to herself.

Anna was also awake and heard the whisper beside her: 'Yes, it has.'

'Oh, you're awake?'

Then, continuing her thought, she added, 'They'll go.'

She did not say what would go, but the other voice knew what she meant.

'They will.'

They stayed awake then, their ears pricked, in case the weather proved propitious and brought them the sound of anchors lifting—the distant sounds of travel.

CHAPTER TWELVE

The return of the prisoner

Early one morning, when they saw the forest of masts again at St Nicholas, Anna said, 'I would so love to go over to the boats and hear some news.'

Then, correcting herself, she said decisively, 'I'm going!'

Her father objected, as his legs would not carry him that far. Her mother also resisted vehemently.

'What will you do there? What will you get out of those onion sellers from the islands?'

Aunt Maria had the fewest objections.

'It's a long way,' she said simply. 'You'll tire yourself out.'

'I won't,' the girl insisted. 'And I won't tire you out either, Father. I'll take Zabeta with me for company.'

She took Fotis' child and they went along the seashore.

The sun was bright, but there was a strong wind that lifted their skirts and played in their hair. There were moments when they could not walk for the driving wind. But they struggled on, rousing all their strength. They felt a rush of joy.

Anna hugged Zabeta, pulled her along and shouted triumphantly, 'Onwards, Zabeta! Onwards! We're going to learn news of Andreas and Angelos! You'll see what wonderful things they will bring us both when they come! You'll see what Andreas will bring!'

Zabeta gritted her teeth and ran, dishevelled and mad with joy, without understanding anything of the unknown boy and what he would bring.

They passed the salt pans and arrived at the turn of the bay. Up until there everything was familiar. Beyond was unknown territory.

A small hill studded with pine trees rose before them. They found the path that led through the woods to the strip of St Nicholas. Anna hesitated for a moment. She had been told to take this path to save time—and because the coastline beyond was precipitous.

'What do you think, Zabeta?'

'Whatever you want, Miss Anna.'

'Well, I think we should be brave. And when Andreas comes we'll tell him, and he'll be pleased.'

She took the little girl off the path and they started to climb over the rocks on the seashore. She felt her blood stirring inside her and her youth, so oppressed at home, gushing out. When Zabeta put a foot wrong or had difficulty in climbing, Anna turned and pulled her up, clasping her warm, childish body close.

'We'll do this journey again together, when he comes,' she said to herself joyfully. 'He will play the seasoned hero, and I'll make him climb over the rocks!'

Desolation reigned over the sky and sea. Desolation was also in the small coves they found from step to step. These were places where the sea went deep into the rocks. Anna and Zabeta sat before the caves, looking at the water gleaming green in the dark cavities. They listened to the hollow sound made by the water striking the cave walls as its power ebbed. Water dripped from a cave roof, and when their ears became accustomed to it they heard this clear sound of eternity. They awaited the drops they would hear when the noise surrounding them had died down, in the great spaces between one lapping of water and the next.

'Now!... Now! Listen!' Anna whispered, clasping the child to her.

They fell silent, waiting until the drop fell from the cave roof onto the green water, its voice merging with the ocean, which came here to breathe its last.

They found unexplored creeks: no one had reason to wander onto this precipitous coastline. The shingle and sand were glowing, worked for thousands of years by the sea. And the shells, plied by the same force, had taken the colour and aspect of those small stones.

An indefinable emotion had spread through Anna's heart, as if theirs were the first human feet to tread these parts. She remembered the books of her childhood, the stories her father had told her about deeds of good people, about journeys and explorations in un-known, far-flung countries, back when they reckoned courage as a force for civilization, for noble actions and for the justification of the human race. They would go to the closest inhabited land near the Poles, climb into a bubble full of air, with no rudder, cut the rope that tied it to the earth, and the freezing air lifted them up and sucked them in, above the white desert, for their final voyage.

'Do you know what those people were looking for?' Dimitris Venis had asked the stunned girl.

'No, Father,' she replied, unable to grasp a rational purpose behind such mad acts of daring.

'Serenity...' he said, moved by the examples of a passion that also burned inside *him*, but was spent on small fantasies, for his weak build was not made of the stuff that could attain such heights. Thus he could only live vicariously the pleasure of the passion that blessed others. He was constrained by that final boundary of the weak and humble.

'Poor Father...' whispered Anna, trying to reconcile it all: their hostile home life, her mother, her father, the roses, Aunt Maria's delving into the past, serenity.

They turned the corner of a steep headland and came face to face with an untraversable wall. It was a huge cliff, around fifty metres high, hanging directly above the sea. A couple of seabirds flew screeching out of high caves. Beside them the world had disappeared. It was as though they had suddenly been isolated by the force of a hostile power.

'What on earth is this?' wondered Anna in hushed tones, dazzled. 'Who would imagine…?'

It was a wild point of the coast, completely different from its general character: one of the contradictions of the Attic landscape.

Zabeta had stopped, perplexed, and was looking up at the cliff. Another bird flew off with a squawk.

'I'm scared… Let's go back, Miss Anna.'

She held the child close. For a moment the thought of danger also went through her mind and she too wanted to turn back. But she would then have to admit to herself that she had not attained her small goal— and young Anna was not merely the daughter of Dimitris Venis: she also held within her, fully formed, the same longings and fantasies.

She examined the place. Only on one section of the cliff did the vertical slope become gentler. There were a few branches too, sticking out of the crevices at irregular intervals.

'Hold my hand!' Anna said with conviction to the child.

She hauled herself up the slope, stretching one hand in front and pulling Zabeta up with the other. They advanced like this slowly and silently. To avoid becoming dizzy, they did not look behind them. At last they reached the top of the cliff. Only then did they turn and look around. They cried out in wonder.

Beyond the southern headland, the most distant place you could see from Anavyssos, they saw, for the first time, a mountain that dropped down to the sea. Behind that lay Cape Sounion. The cape was not visible, but they could see the island of San Giorgi, that huge caterpillar floating in the Aegean.

They turned to look west. The forest of masts in the anchorage of St Nicholas was beneath them. They could see the crews coming and going, wrapped in their blankets, and hear their voices. The strong wind blew through the girls' hair, giving them the measure of the devil that a sail would have to contend with on the open sea.

'See? We're here, Zabeta! We're here!'

A sense of triumph shone in her clear eyes. And suddenly Anna Venis, wind-beaten on the summit by gusts that howled as if they wanted to whisk her away, saw how calm it was at the end of her quest and what serenity there was, deep inside her body.

They bounded down towards the anchorage.

'Let's go back, Zabeta! Quick! Quick!'

They bid goodbye to the sailors and hastened to leave. This time they took the path that skirted the cliff and went to Anavyssos through the small forest on the hills.

'If only you understood what news we're bringing, Zabeta!' said Anna, out of breath.

'But we didn't even get to the white church!' the child ventured to say. 'Wasn't that why we were going?'

She did not feel they had reached their goal without accomplishing that: getting to the white speck they had seen for so long, ever since they had come to Anavyssos. Why had they not gone there?

'I'll take you another time!' said Anna. 'Now our journey has ended.'

They kept running.

Emerging from the forest, they ended up in a bare place from where they could see the shacks of Anavyssos. At some point on the footpath they came to a well. The place was so dry and this well was a new discovery of the journey.

They halted.

'I wonder if it has water.'

'I'm thirsty,' said the little girl, panting.

'So am I.'

They leaned over the well. In the serene depths was a dark, motionless mass. They threw in a stone and waited a few seconds. The muffled clang of disturbed water resounded. Anna turned to the child and kissed her on the cheek.

'There's water,' she said.

Beside the well a large tree trunk had been hollowed out with a broad tool to make a trough. The shepherds took their sheep there to water them. There was also a bucket on a bristling rope for humans.

They hauled up some brackish water and drank. It calmed them somewhat, and abated the mad excitement of the return.

'Let's sit down for a moment,' said Zabeta.

'Of course.'

A deep tenderness overflowed in Anna. She felt it as a coolness running over her body. She lay on her back and closed her eyes. The wind was still blowing strong, and the roar of the sea came from afar, harsh and certain. The sound of the nearby forest faded in this certainty; everything faded. Over the waves travelled the fate of the world. Lord, let him come. Let him come as he should. Let him be what he should. Here the earth is waterless and the land is covered by clouds of sand raised by the winds. The seeds sown by the refugees still have not grown. Only the huge salt pyramids disturb the silence of the enclosed space. From here—which once was a refuge for the dead—from this country of tombs, some of the living are begging You to show Your mercy. Here is Anna, little Anna. Come, even if just for her. She is very young. Come and topple the white salt pyramids, bring down the clouds of sand. Send a man.

'Are you crying?' asked Zabeta, looking at the girl's face in surprise.

Anna wiped her face quickly with her palm, scattering the wet beads over it.

'There's sand in my eye,' she said.

The news flooded the small settlement of Phocians.

'The prisoners are coming back! The prisoners are coming back! Anna Venis brought the news from the ships at St Nicholas! Out at sea they came upon the boats making for Piraeus!'

The news spread through the small plain, around the hills, to the people stooped in their toil over the earth.

'They're coming back!'

'They're coming back!'

The oxen stopped pulling the plough and turned their bitter eyes slowly to east and west. The iron tools fell from human hands. The pit they were digging remained open. The sheep rose from the blessed stillness of noon. Everything—men, iron, animals—rushed downhill, drawn by a magnetic force.

'They're coming back!'

Every shack was waiting for someone from the East. They were stunned by the news. In the house of Doctor Venis, the flurry of joy had left its mark on everything: the face of the half-blind woman, Aunt Maria, Dimitris' hands, the blood in the girl's veins. Everything. Only on Irini's face had the icy stillness not moved, except indefinably. She was evidently participating only from obligation.

'Tell me again, dear,' Aunt Maria said to Anna, radiant with joy. 'How did they tell you? Is it certain?'

And Anna said again how they had told her on the anchored ships. One of them, out on the open sea, had come upon the boat carrying the prisoners. They had even exchanged words.

Night fell. From outside the windows came the murmur of people wandering around, unable to stay
cooped up in the shacks, discussing the news and
making plans.

'I'm going out,' said Anna.

'I see no reason,' said her mother. 'It's chilly.'

'Leave the girl alone!' the doctor intervened. 'She's
the hero of the hour!'

People were discussing the news in small groups.
The women had gathered separately and the children
were running around and whooping. From the fireplaces thin lines of smoke made their lonely way up
above the din.

Anna arrived breathlessly at the shack of Andreas'
mother. She put her ear to the door. There was silence
inside, but the door was ajar. She pushed it open and
went in. A small passage led to the bedroom on the left
and the kitchen with its low fireplace on the right. It
did not have a wooden floor. The limy earth smelled
tidy, lonely.

The girl hesitated. Her eyes gradually became
accustomed to the half-darkness. She looked into the
bedroom. A shadowy body was standing still. She
recognised the thin shape of the simple, troubled
woman, praying with her face turned towards the
east.

She tiptoed closer. Aunt Sophia, absorbed, did not
notice the tiny sound. Anna stopped just behind her.

She heard clearly the whispered supplication:

'Thou hast proved mine heart; thou hast visited me in the night; thou hast tried me, and shalt find nothing; I am purposed that my mouth shall not transgress. Concerning the works of men, by the word of thy lips I have kept me from the paths of the destroyer.'[8]

There was a shuffling of feet.

'Who is it?' the frightened voice of Andreas' mother asked into the darkness.

'It's me,' the young voice replied.

'My dear,' said Aunt Sophia with emotion, recognising the girl. 'How good you are… Let me turn on the light.'

'Don't worry, Aunt Sophia. It's fine like this.'

She called her 'aunt,' and she could not clearly distinguish the personality of this aunt from her real aunt, Maria. Merely that the former was more simple.

Anna said, 'Now you will be able to rest. You have suffered all these storms alone.'

The old woman took the hands of the girl and squeezed them.

'My sweet girl! I will tell him when he comes. I will tell him that you came to our shack at this hour…'

Yes, Aunt Sophia will tell her son that Anna came at this hour, when life felt lonelier than ever precisely because she could now, finally, hear his footsteps.

---

[8] Psalm 17

'What joy you brought us today, my dear! And to your house, with your poor Aunt Maria… What joy has arrived!'

'It is time he came,' said Anna softly, her voice trembling.

'Who are you talking about?'

She hesitated.

'About joy, Aunt Sophia.'

'Do you think they were together all the time they were away?' asked Andreas' mother. 'I mean, him and Angelos…'

'Who knows but God?'

A moment passed. Then Anna asked timidly, 'Are you… are you afraid at all, Aunt Sophia?'

'In God's name, why should I be afraid? I've prayed so much.'

She had an extraordinary certainty, a firm belief even amid the fearful rumours circulating about those who had stayed in the East following the disaster of 1922.

'Why do you ask?' she said.

'Because I am also certain…'

'Is your aunt not certain about Angelos?'

'My aunt is a different person,' said Anna.

A moment passed.

'I prepared this today,' said Andreas' mother.

Only then, wanting to show what 'this' was, did she notice that it was still dark.

'I'll turn on the light,' she said.

She went to light the humble tin lamp and brought it into the room where the girl was waiting.

'Look Anna, I prepared his suit. Here it is. It's the only thing of his I brought from home.'

Hanging behind the door, freshly ironed, was his light grey suit.

Anna got up and went over slowly to where this sign of tenderness was hanging. She stroked it with the tips of her fingers.

'It's a cheerful colour,' she said.

'He always liked light colours. He has a good heart. The two of you…'

She paused.

'The two of you are very good friends, you and Andreas. Isn't that right, Anna?'

'Yes, we are very good friends.'

'Well, from now on you won't be on your own here, my dear.'

Anna rose abruptly.

'Good night, Aunt Sophia.'

'Good night, my dear. May God be with you. Thank you.'

When she arrived home, late, her mother scolded her, saying, 'Where have you been all this time?'

'I thought Aunt Sophia would be alone. I went to keep her company in her joy,' she explained.

'And you thought it so necessary to go?'

'Why do you say that?' interrupted Dimitris, vexed. 'It was a lovely thought to go and see a lonely mother.'

He turned to his daughter: 'Well Anna, how was Sophia?'

'She was praying. She was happy. Waiting...'

'So, everyone is waiting,' said Irini stonily.

'Yes, Mother, everyone is waiting,' replied Anna in the same tone.

Then, not seeing her aunt in the room, she asked after her: 'Where is Aunt Maria?'

'She's been in your room since you left.'

Anna ran up to their room and opened the door. She hesitated.

Absorbed in her task, the half-blind woman was running her hands over something.

'What are you doing, Aunt?'

'Come in, Anna,' she said. 'I am preparing his suit.'

'Oh, darling Aunt!'

And, unable to endure the emotions of that day any longer, she burst into tears.

A day passed over Anavyssos, then a night. Then another day, then more days and more nights.

No news came from the circle of hills, from where they were expecting those who were to return to appear. The oxen slowly started pulling the plough again over the earth. Lights were lit and extinguished early in the Phocians' shacks. The smoke from their fireplaces rose as lonely as ever. And the suits of Andreas and Angelos remained hanging, untouched, waiting to clothe their bodies.

Until, one afternoon, the land filled with the cry, 'They're coming on the path! The prisoners are coming! The prisoners!'

Who was the first to give the cry? All the men in the village, all the women and children, rushed towards the path leading to the hills. They ran screaming, each treading on the other's heels and trying to get past. The salt pyramids lost their severity and smiled at the comic sight.

'What is it?' one pyramid asked.

'They're playing,' said another.

Anna was at the rocks of Thymari. But the doctor was among the crowd that was 'playing'.

The Phocians, out of breath, were approaching the upper village where the other refugees had settled, when they stopped all of a sudden.

Just one person emerged on the path. His body was covered in sacks, his face was yellow, and dogs were yapping at his heels. Behind him were the hills.

The shadow of death loomed over the crowd of Phocians, until one awestruck voice said, 'Look!'

And the person kept coming, along with the dogs and the hills. Then they heard a murmur, and the voice of the wanderer, asking, 'Is my mother here?'

Recognising his voice, the whole crowd fell on him, shouting, 'It's Andreas! It's Sophia's Andreas!'

They inundated him with questions.

'Have you seen so-and-so? Have you seen so-and-so?'

Under the wave of people, like a frightened animal, he muttered, as if asking for mercy, 'I know nothing… I know nothing…'

They descended on Anavyssos together. The prisoner went first and the crowd followed. Dimitris was at his side, out of breath.

'Is it far?' Andreas asked the doctor in desperation at one point. 'In God's name, let's get there! Let's get there!'

'We'll be there soon, child,' said the doctor. 'Look, there are our shacks. Now, could you give the people a yes or a no if you have seen any of their family?'

A yes or a no—how simple everything is here.

'Is Anna alive?' the young man asked after a while.

'Yes, she is. She is here. So is Angelos' mother. You were together when they caught you, weren't you?'

The young man made a violent movement, as if starting from a nightmare.

'What did you say?' he said rudely.

'I was asking about my nephew, Angelos. Will he be on the next boat?'

The questioning voice is calm, serene. How can the people here ask such things so simply and calmly?

'Will he come on the next boat?' the voice persisted.

Again, 'Will he come?'

The harsh voice of the young man, which he was unable to contain any longer, broke into pieces: 'No! No! He won't come! He won't come! Stop asking now!' he cried in despair.

He sat on the ground and held his face in his hands. They all then made a voiceless circle over this apparition.

'Who is he talking about?' they asked under their breath.

The doctor begged them to widen the circle and give the boy some space. He knelt down beside him and held his forehead, as if checking for a fever.

Then he leaned closer to the young man's ear, entreating. 'His mother... must find out nothing, nothing...' he whispered, trembling. 'She must wait for him.'

Andreas lowered his head to the ground, slightly calmer now.

'She will not find out.'

PART TWO

CHAPTER ONE

Fairy tale of 1922

More days and nights passed over the hills of Anavyssos. Life found its course again, and the salt pyramids their composure. 'Did something happen?' asked one of them. 'No, nothing,' responded the other. 'They were playing.'

'Well then, what do you know?' the villagers asked Andreas, their tone of voice showing their indignation at his silence.

'Nothing,' he responded. 'I know nothing.'

'Were you alone there?'

'Yes.'

All of them said that the boy was not in his right mind.

Aunt Maria was sitting at the window. Next to her sat her son's friend. The days had begun to improve. Evening was falling over the sea of Anavyssos and the mountain of Aegina. The eyes of Aunt Maria were focused on a point beyond the window, and her figure was darkening, becoming one with the approaching evening.

'It's two months today…' she said softly.

'Since when?' asked Andreas inattentively, in the same tone.

'Since you came. See how you've stopped counting the days?'

He felt a deep shame, as her words contained such bitterness.

'I have been waiting like you,' he said. 'You are his mother, but I am like a brother to him. We were so close over there.'

'I didn't mean to suggest anything,' she said to calm him. 'Only that the days pass so quickly. That's all I meant.'

Her voice had taken a deep note, heavy with perseverance, becoming more downcast as time went on. She no longer sobbed as she had done when Andreas first came back. Nonetheless, when the two of them were alone together and she looked at him, her eyes often filled with tears.

'The summer days must have been interminable,' Aunt Maria said.

'It was not so bad. Where we worked, on the farm, we would wake up early, dig and water. Nearby there was a stream to which birds flocked to drink. They let us put up nets to catch them. Angelos enjoyed that game a lot. That's how the days went by. The nights in the barn were long, though.'

'In the barn?' Aunt Maria stopped him.

'I mean… the first days on the farm… they put us in a barn.'

'You hadn't told me that,' she said slowly.

He struggled to remember what he had told her. Every time they spoke he mixed something up. He could not keep in order everything he had said to comfort her.

'Don't imagine that it was horrid,' Andreas tried to explain. 'Angelos and I talked about it. We were very comfortable in the barn. But when the summer nights came, we asked them to let us sleep outside. We slept under a great plane tree and listened to the sound of the running water. It was truly peaceful. Angelos found his passion for the night sky again. He taught me to find Sirius, and the Great Bear… Remember how we loved astronomy at school!'

'Was your guard sleeping at that time?' asked Aunt Maria.

'We had no guard. We were alone.'

'Last time you told me that was the worst thing: someone shadowing you day and night…'

'Oh, that was in the camp!' he fervently assured her. 'No, on the farm we were free. We had a good time. They were fond of us. When we fell asleep, it was a deep, calm and dreamless sleep.'

'How strange that is for Angelos,' his mother said. 'He always dreamed the most unlikely and incomprehensible dreams. They were like fairy tales when he told them to me.'

She paused, before asking abruptly, 'Did he not tell you any of his dreams, all that time?'

A shudder rose inside him, passing through his entire body. He returned at once to his friend's last night, on a wild, pine-covered mountainside, where Angelos dreamed his last dream. He was, he said, with two friends, walking over endless fire. Then the earth opened and they fell in. They kept falling. They were wondering among themselves about the depth of the earth. And suddenly their clothes were filled, inundated, crammed with sky, pure sky. It was like golden mud. They touched it, stroked it with their eyes and fingers...

It was the dream of Angelos' last night, and he had told it to Andreas a few hours before his end.

And now Angelos' mother was sitting opposite him and asking him calmly, 'Did he not tell you any of his dreams, all that time?'

He tried to gather his strength so his voice would not tremble.

'No, he did not tell me a single dream.'

Night was well advanced. Aunt Maria remained silent, her eyes fixed on the starry sky. At one moment she seemed to fall asleep—she was so still. But then her voice asked again, softly, 'Can you show me, child, roughly where Sirius is? I cannot see anything anymore.'

The star shone clearly, as if washed by heavy rain.

'There it is.'

Absorbed and silent, she looked for a long time to where he was pointing.

'Shall I turn on a light?' Andreas asked after a while.

She did not respond. He got up and lit the lowly lamp. The beams cast their desolation throughout the whole room, their great shadows falling everywhere.

'Good night.'

'Good night, my dear.'

As he was leaving he met Anna at the front door. He could not quite make out her expression, but from the sound of her voice she seemed upset.

'I was waiting for you on the rocks, on the path to Thymari,' she said. 'Why didn't you come?'

'It's not my fault,' he replied. 'Aunt Maria kept me.'

She crossed her arms nervily, saying nothing. Then she said in a low voice, 'I was also waiting for you to come back, you know.'

'Don't get upset, Anna. I cannot disappoint her.'

She took his arm with sudden tenderness.

'Do you want to walk down to the salt pans?'

No, tonight he would not. He was utterly exhausted. Tomorrow, he pleaded.

'My God! Try to start saying yes again!' A knot tightened her voice. 'Goodnight.'

She hurried out of sight through the open door.

When he returned to their shack he looked dead on his feet. So it was every day. It was a terrible duty, recurring every evening as night was closing in. In the first days of his return it was so agonising that he tried to avoid it. Then he gradually became used to it, saw it as an obligation. You can get used to anything. You can become used to looking inside yourself and seeing how naked and desolate it is, as if you are the first on the earth and beginning the history of mankind, now and alone. You become used to believing in nothing, not dreaming, denuded of everything that reconciles us with people and life. You become used to destroying yourself and others, and everything inside you becoming silent—fear, imagination, pity. Everything, therefore, is simply a matter of degree: until you fall. Thus you can grow used to this, too: telling stories to a mother every day about a child who will not return.

'His mother must not find out anything,' Dimitris had pleaded with him again. 'She can wait all her remaining years without yielding. But if she has nothing to wait for, she cannot.'

Therefore, so that this mother would find out nothing, Andreas sat and told her a story. It was a fairy tale, all colour and emotion, full of kindliness, about two lads who found themselves in the turbulence of war. It was full of pious gratitude and fervent tears.

'Angelos will come with the next dispatch, or the next, or the next. He'll come,' were his first words to his friend's mother.

Then, when they were left alone the same evening in her room, Aunt Maria made him tell her everything from the beginning, blow by blow, about how they spent their days—fourteen months—of imprisonment.

His own mother, Aunt Sophia, was also beside him. She must also hear the fairy tale and nothing else. He improvised what had happened and the harsh lines evaporated, as happens with the fairy tales of dragons and monsters that you tell a child to make them sleep. The night is calm, and an angel sits beside them, pouring the light of its face over the eyes of the child, waiting for the time to come to close them. Everything is calm, the dragons and monsters disappear gradually in this warm light, become confused, take indefinite forms; the child smiles and his eyes slowly close. The child falls asleep. Peace be with him! A mother must sleep too. God be with her!

Well, the fairy tale that Andreas told to Aunt Maria went like this—

On the great march into the Anatolian heartland, they were always walking through great forests, with waterfalls and shadowy gorges. Since they had no forests where they lived, apart from the olive groves, they were overcome by a strange fear, but also a curious enchantment. Unknown birds of astonishing colour flew around them and, in the evening when the sun set, the shadows lengthened as far as the eye could see. They camped in the forests and gorges, wherever night found them. When the first stars came out, the forest filled with the calls of wild animals emerging from their nests to find food. The prisoners were not afraid, as they lit great fires to protect themselves. The flames leapt high, and the branches of the age-old trees leaned over them, as if invoking the holy flame to take them, to bring them peace; they had lived a lot and waited a lot. The animals did not come near: the young men only heard their calls, until these, too, gradually died away. They died down to a soft moan, soft and almost human, which fastened onto the leaves and the firm trunks, onto the air and the people, making them sleep.

Those were the nights. In the days, on the march, they stopped at clear running water where they drank, and at sheepfolds and huts.

The villagers offered them bread and milk, then they came to their doorways to wish them Godspeed. These villagers did not know if there was still war or if it was over. They knew nothing. They knew only that people were looking for bread, and they gave it with the simplicity possessed of great deeds.

They spent one night in a village that clung to a pine-clad mountain. From there, at its great altitude, they saw the sea for the last time.

The sun was falling when someone turned around and saw it. It was a long, serene layer, a strip just visible through the opening of the mountain.

'Lads,' said their comrade. 'The sea!'

All of them then turned towards that fleeting line, which would soon disappear from their eyes forever.

They looked down. It was windy and the sea would be choppy, with its succession of waves going up and down. So they imagined. But not the smallest movement reached their fixated eyes. Nothing. The sea remained still, with its great streaked lines, which must be its waves—also still, bored.

That was their only bitterness, after all the marching. But when they entered the village in the forest, the women were quick to offer them food. They put the young men in a large hut, brought hot, homemade *trachanas*, and let them eat. They also brought torches and lit them, as the night was cold. Andreas slept beside Angelos and, always in each other's arms, they fell into blessed, undisturbed sleep.

'But did these people know nothing about the war?' asked Aunt Maria, moved.

'Oh no, not a thing!' said Andreas, 'It was as if the world had left them behind. As if God Himself had forgotten them. They were simple and good. They lived with their sheep and with the crops that the good earth gave them, and the earth was sprinkled with their sweat. So when we, in our sorry state, suddenly landed in this peace and quiet, we were like beings sent by the Prophet to test whether the villagers' hearts remained clean and spotless.'

The two mothers, Andreas' and Angelos', were sitting and weeping as the fairy tale unfolded. They were tears of gratitude to humanity, which had remained good.

'When the march finished, we found work on the trains,' he continued. 'We emptied coaches loaded with cereals. That was easy work. Then they took us to a village. It was winter then and the first snow had fallen. In that village one day, a doctor called Kamil Bey came and found us in our hideaway. He called us out and gave us warm clothes. He asked us what we did in our homeland, and we told him we were still at school. He too was a young lad—he had just finished his studies—and the three of us became like brothers.

'Then we left again and found work on a farm. Things were relaxed there, as if there was no war. We could pray, if we wanted. We could sing. No one stood in our way. When the owners came to hunt wild boar, they took us with them into the scrubland. There, in that quiet corner, we found peace. I was taken on the first dispatch to Greece. Angelos was going to come on the next, or the one after.'

When he said goodbye to Angelos, his friend's last words were to go to his mother and give her his greetings. He went with Angelos to the tomb of one of their companions, who had died peacefully on one of the final days of summer. There was nothing particularly wrong with him, he just had an inexplicable melancholy. They had buried him near a stream, under a poplar. The oleanders bent their branches beside him, and at dusk gave him shade. At the place where Andreas bid a final goodbye to their dead friend, at his tomb, he also bid goodbye to Angelos. 'Send my greetings to my mother and tell her that I am well and will not be long.'

. . . .

So ended the fairy tale. Andreas was afraid that the two mothers would not believe him. The newspapers were full of terrible stories. From mouth to mouth, the legend of the East was struggling to find its form in the imagination of people who had not experienced it.

That is why Andreas was afraid that Aunt Maria would not believe him. But it seems that his voice was compelling. Moreover, one can bear suffering if there is hope. That is, perhaps, the clearest understanding of the future.

'How differently we imagined it,' his friend's mother merely said. 'Everyone was saying…'

'People imagine things,' he replied. 'The problem was that we could not write to you. Otherwise you would have known.'

'Yes,' she said. 'The silence was terrible.'

Andreas lay down on the soft mattress that his mother had prepared for him and closed his eyes. In the darkness he heard her tiptoeing in the bedroom so as not to make a noise. Then he heard a gentle murmur. He opened his eyes a moment. In the candlelight that seeped in from the passage he could see her praying in front of the icons. This lasted a long while. His ear just caught a whisper: 'To you I commit my every hope, Mother of God. Guard me and keep me.'

Silence. She seemed to have finished. He heard her footsteps coming closer. She thought he was asleep. She leaned over him, her warm breath touching his face. Her fingers gently caressed his forehead. He could not endure this tender touch, and opened his eyes.

'Weren't you asleep?' she said, surprised, in her calm voice.

'No, Mother, I'm still awake.'

She remained silent a moment. Then she brought her fingers to his face again and stroked it.

Unconsciously, he moved to guard himself from this tenderness. He felt afraid. After the gruelling times he had lived through, he feared his fate as if it were sitting close by him, lurking, waiting.

But his mother was a simple person. She did not know anything of what he knew about people, even at his tender age. May she remain like that, until God calls her.

'You seem to have changed slightly,' was all she said.

'No!' he assured her. Nothing had changed.

'I am just a year older. That's all, Mother.'

She leaned over him. Her voice was softer, and he could barely hear her. 'Is it true what you told me about your time over there, and about Angelos?' she asked, desperately trying to guess the reason for his suffering.

'Why would it not be? You remember that since I was a child I couldn't tell lies.'

She did not dare to express any more suspicion. She slowly raised her head from his.

'It's alright,' she said to him. 'I did not mean to suggest anything.'

From the window of the shack Andreas could see the stars trembling. He remembered another night, the last he had spent with his mother, in a basement, before the enemy took him from her arms. He remembered what the stars looked like then through the skylight. He remembered too that a mouse was screeching, and that he was still afraid of mice then. He had been resting his head on his mother's lap, her warm breath touching his face like a living substance, just as now. So, nothing had changed. Merely that now he could not rest on her like a child—that was over.

'It's late, Mother,' he said to her. 'You should rest.'

She covered his arms, which were outside the blankets, and went away slowly.

Then, when he was left alone in the night, they began to come: Angelos, Orestes, little Zach the Armenian, all the companions he had lost. Their pale, anguished faces were motionless, and their large childlike eyes remained fixed on him, as if asking why he had abandoned them. The hair on Angelos' head was ruffled, and a slender strip of red ran a zigzag down his cheek, dripping.

He covered himself completely, clasped his hands together—the fingers that had held the hands of his friend in his final hour. And now he was telling fairy tales to the mother of the dead boy, talking about catching birds with nets, and that he sent his greetings to her and would come soon. Oh Angelos, how fine it would be if we were all together again here! We could really go catching birds by day, and at night you would show us Sirius and the Great Bear. Then we would sit our little blond Zach at the piano to play music—that deep and incomprehensible power that shakes the waters, moves the winds and clouds and lulls the hearts of men. And when he has nothing more to say on his instrument, when he has given with all his might, then again there would be something unsaid, and the human voice would come to complete it. Then Zach would sing to us songs of his distant Armenia. His warm, childish voice would sing of the dense forests, where the sun does not touch the ground, of the mountains, which are always covered in snow and mist, of the waters that run to unknown seas. Then his voice would grow softer, and he would sing of the troubles of the people, that beleaguered race which ceaselessly sheds its blood, colouring the streams. That is what his warm, youthful voice would sing. And we would feel a sacred power rising in our chests to do great deeds, good works for people and life. We were still owed time to be children—you too, Angelos, and you, Zach, and me alongside you. But now I do not even know if you have the quietness of the earth to cover you, or if the jackals of the desert have eaten you.

And I sit here and tell fairy tales to your mothers, and when my own comes to stroke me I shiver and am afraid, as if death is approaching.

. . . .

His mother was leaning over him, terrified. His body was still shaking with sobbing. The pillow was soaked with tears. It was the middle of the night.

'What is it, child?' she said. 'What is it, in God's name? Just when you're back...'

She spoke, and her eyes also began to weep.

Tired, devoid of strength, he turned over and rested on her.

'Yes, Mother, a little more like that. A little more.'

CHAPTER TWO

*A woman from the East struggles to reconcile herself
with the sea*

It rained all night, but the next morning the sun had
come out.

'I'm going to Zabeta's,' Anna said to her mother.

'Well, you *could* stay at home sometimes,' she re-
torted. 'You're always out for no reason.'

'I do what I can, Mother, at home. I can't do any
more.'

'That's no way to talk, Anna. I think you have
changed a lot recently.'

'Oh, for God's sake, Mother! Stop pestering me!'

Anna had felt her severe gaze more and more. She
thought she could even discern a certain hostility in it,
although she shrank from the thought. She was very
young and it was not easy for her to see into that bitter,
entrapped life. Only this was certain: every passing day
bound her, Anna, closer to her father and distanced
her from her mother. And the circle around Irini Venis
became smaller.

'Goodbye!' said Anna, and left without another word.

She did not go directly to Zabeta's. She veered off to Andreas' shack. She found him in the garden with his mother, digging the wet earth.

'Good morning, Anna.'

'I was going to Zabeta's, but I thought I would come by here to see how you are. What rain we had last night!'

She looked at her friend's face. From his pallor she could tell he had had a bad night. He tried to avoid her searching glance.

'Yes, it was a terrible night,' he said. 'I couldn't sleep at all.'

'Do you want to come to Zabeta's? I feel so sorry for her new mother. She is so alone.'

'Go on,' agreed Aunt Sophia, 'you go too. That woman is now one of ours. Go and see her.'

He put down his spade and washed his hands.

'Let's go, Anna.'

On the road she said:

'My family were very fond of Eleni, who was taken by the rain. And her husband. Well, my father mainly. He thinks he has the "precious essence"—imagination—inside him.'

'Well, they're cast in the same mould, that's why.'

'Oh yes! Every brightness in our house is born of my father's dreams. I think he taught me, too, to believe. To believe in his rose garden. That's why...'

She paused.

'That's why…?' Andreas asked.

'That's why I'm afraid.'

And since she saw no movement in his face with which to divine his thoughts, she asked him, 'And you… do you believe in all that?'

A light shudder passed across the lines of his face: 'Don't ask me that, Anna.'

Then he said wearily, 'I cannot be like you two anymore.'

They had reached Fotis' shack. An area of about an acre of ploughed land spoke of human toil. The wall surrounding the plot of land was made from the rocks they had cleared. A huge mass of useless stones was piled up on one side. Fotis had dug deeply here too for water, made a well and onto it had fastened the posts of a windmill. They were made from oak branches, hardened over a flame, and the sails were of new calico. From afar it looked like a toy. It was, however, a genuinely practical device, dressed in a toy's beauty, a beauty synonymous with pure joy.

'Oh, look down there, the Phocians are playing!' shouted one of the shepherds up on the mountain, on the first day the white mill had started to turn.

'They're destitute and they're still playing!' said another.

'They're different people. We won't be able to touch them,' a third concluded, involuntarily admiring the toy with its white blades.

But when one day the Arvanites came down and saw the mill close to, they said, 'Oh, it's not a toy.'

'It is a toy!' answered Fotis. 'But… it also pulls up a bit of water.'

They were perplexed when they saw the great tank next to it, filling up drop by drop with water the 'toy' brought up from the depths of the earth.

'In winter there's all the water you can ask for,' explained Fotis. 'But as you say, my good sirs, your land drives away the clouds when they're needed. Well, this little toy spreads its sails and plays God.'

'These are different people,' the lords of the mountain concluded in their wisdom, resigned to their fate.

'Wasn't it wonderful that Fotis thought of that?' Anna said to Andreas.

'It was useful.'

'Oh don't *you* look at everything like that too! Just like my mother…'

He was going to say, 'That's how I was brought up,' but at that moment they heard Zabeta's voice, shouting into the shack: 'It's Miss Anna! The young lady is coming!'

An old man was sitting at the door of the shack. He was rolling a cigarette, absorbed in his task. Behind him emerged Vaso, Fotis' new wife, holding a child by the hand, and then Fotis' two younger children.

'Sit down, sit down,' Vaso said respectfully to the two young people, looking at the ground. 'The master will be here right away.'

From her accent you could tell that she was from the Turkish-speaking parts.

'It's the *dochtor's* daughter,' she explained to her father in Turkish, 'and the lad who came from the East.'

'Welcome!' said the old man, before returning to his tobacco.

'Well, tell us then, Vaso, are you happy you came to us?' asked Anna.

'God is great and good,' she replied, not venturing to judge His deeds.

'But why don't you come down to the seashore on Sundays with the other women? You're like a scared deer.'

'There's a lot to do in the house. All of these ones…'

She pointed at the four children: one of her own, who she had brought with her, and the three of Fotis and Eleni.

When the winter days had worsened and the white blades of the windmill went up over the well, Fotis had realised how alone he was and how much toil there was in life. He now had three fields to look after: the field of the little god where Eleni was buried, one in Thymari and one here at the shack. Woman is the ox of the house, he thought. At night he felt a tingling come over him and, asleep, his hands would reach out unconsciously to seek the warm body of the woman taken by the rain. He had not touched a woman since then: it would not have been acceptable to do so in their village, and on his trips to Aegina he had other cares. One day, therefore, he woke up and thought, I need a woman here.

He thought through the young Phocian women one by one, but was not satisfied: 'I need a seasoned woman.'

His mind went to the upper village, to the Turkish speakers.

Fotis was full of admiration for what they had accomplished in only a few months. All the mountains around, which were just pastureland before, were now ploughed. Every day Fotis would see the terraces of cultivated land rising higher, while the rocky corridors beside them were left fallow. The terraces seemed to him to be carved out by their very nails, fixed marks of people climbing upwards.

The marks kept climbing, up to the summit, never down to the sea. They fear it like the devil, Fotis concluded, as he went to look for a new wife among them, in place of the one who had been swept away.

Thus Vaso came to his shack. She was still a young woman, with a small boy from her first husband who had been killed at Çanakkale, and her old father. At first, when she came to the shack in Anavyssos, the first days after her marriage to Fotis, she was like a scared rabbit. The sea rumbled, advancing to a few metres from the door of their shack, and the waves broke on the great strand with a deep roar. It was as if a furious hand clasped her heart and body and did not let her rest.

'What's wrong?' Fotis asked severely, waking in the night and seeing her lying awake next to him, eyes wide open.

'Nothing,' she replied.

Women in her position were not to complain about their fate.

'What's wrong?' persisted Fotis, more aggressively. 'Speak!'

Eventually, forced to give in, she pointed to the sea and said, 'That!'

Fotis, not understanding, rolled over and went to sleep.

Vaso, however, remained awake that night and many others. On those nights there came, one by one, memories from the high, snowy mountains of her homeland on the border of Iran. Their hut had been on one of those mountains. When she was still young, one night she heard human footsteps outside. Who could it be? Only shepherds from time to time ended up in that wilderness. But even that was a rarity.

'Who is it?' cried little Vaso.

'I'm not from here,' said the voice. 'But I am a Christian and I'm lost on the mountain. I'm hungry.'

Vaso strained to see the stranger in the twilight, and then she lowered her eyes.

'Wait.'

She went to milk the goat and returned with the warm milk in a large bowl. She brought bread she had made herself.

'Are you alone?' the stranger asked as he ate.

She was alone then. Her father was grazing their flock in the gorge. There was no one else.

Gradually Vaso became bolder. Her big brown eyes looked at the stranger.

'Where do you come from?' she asked.

He told her he was from far away. But, unable to make her understand, he said, 'From the sea.'

Vaso had never heard of it. She imagined something like a golden sky over the earth.

'No, it's not like that,' laughed the stranger. 'It's water. Wherever your eye looks, it will see water, moving back and forth.'

Vaso was lost in thought for some time, astonished at this strange water-country. She had never left her corner of the mountain. Far off at the end of the plain, she could see the trains going by, bound for central Anatolia. She heard the distant rumble approaching, then it became quiet again and the wind whispered clearly in the leaves of the trees. When she was even younger, they sent her to graze their animals. She was out all day, returning to the pen when the sun began to set. But once she was away for many days and nights with her father and their flock. Then, still a child, she met the silent god of her land, of the great mountain. The first time Vaso made that long journey, the snow had begun to melt. At that season, when the snows are melting, a lake forms on the great mountain. Around it are deep ravines and age-old trees.

Plagued by lightning and wind, they bend as if exhausted. Great waterfalls rush down from on high. You can hear the deep roar of falling water, and from time to time an even wilder din: the uprooted trees brought down by the torrents. One day Vaso, her father and their flock found themselves before a great cave. They gave a loud cry and, from inside, huge black birds and bats with flat wings flew out, squawking fearfully. They circled above, then soared downwards, following the running water. Another day they met bandits in the forest: a wild young man with a thick beard, and his three companions. Each bandit had wrapped a cartridge belt around his waist and crossed it over his chest, and the weapons gleamed in the sun.

They sheltered together all night, lighting a fire and roasting a ram. All four of the bandits had been condemned to death by the government.

Three of them had their spirits up and sang songs of the deeds of the hero Çakiji. Only the dark-skinned young man said nothing. Leaning on his weapons, he gazed up at the night sky. When he had drunk a lot of wine he sang a song with an unfamiliar tune. His was no human voice: the insects fell silent at its song, and so too the leaves that were trembling on the trees.

Vaso never went onto the great mountain again. But she had taken everything that was useful to her. She stayed in their shack and looked at the trains coming and going in the distance like great monsters. She remembered the lake that forms up there when the snows melt, the great tormented trees, the deep caves, the bats, the birds, and the night with the bandits. That was enough. She would remain there in their shack, and at night, every night, she would dream. Until one of the shepherds would come to seek her out to be his wife. Then Vaso would change master. She would go to another hut and, for a time, things would change; then they would be the same again, as calm as before. At night, even dreams—those mystical charms that ease human lives—might come. In her dreams she would see the distant land with the golden sky that the lost stranger had told her about, the water trembling and roaring. And she would have nothing to fear of that distant country, as it was a dream. And dreams ease human lives.

. . . .

'She must have got used to us by now,' Anna said to Fotis, Vaso's new husband.

'Oh yes, Miss Anna. But how queer those people are!'

How queer they are! Vaso was now used to the sea, but she could still not put one single piece of octopus in her mouth.

'Can you believe she doesn't eat seafood!' said Fotis, astonished. 'What strange people!'

One day, Fotis brought up two pen shells from the sea. 'What are those?' Vaso asked fearfully. 'They're out of the ravine behind Thymari,' he joked. 'They're a bit like snails.'

'And what will we do with them?' Vaso asked.

'Eat them!' he said.

'But they smell of the sea!'

'That's because deep in the earth there are veins of water that link up with the sea.'

Vaso thus agreed to put this strange thing in her mouth, as it was a product of the earth.

'What a different world theirs is!' said Fotis again.

Vaso was sitting in the corner, wearing an expression like a scared animal who realises it has misbehaved and awaits its punishment.

'But I didn't tell you!' Fotis said to Andreas and Anna. 'As soon as the weather improves I'm taking her on a journey to Aegina with me. That'll break her bile.'

It was the first time that he had announced this plan, since a husband does not sit and drool over his plans with his wife.

Vaso's face changed colour at once. She clenched her lips in fear, merely saying, 'When do you think this will happen, master?'

'I told you: when the weather improves!'

He liked her expression of complete subjection, and it flattered his pride that she called him 'master'. His first wife, Eleni, was also from the same stock of obedient people. But she had a will that found a way of revealing itself, regardless of whether his will was stronger and subjugated hers in the end. This woman, by contrast, was a faithful, obedient animal. Nothing more.

'Can I come on that trip too?' Andreas asked softly. It was the first thing he had said all this time.

Anna, surprised, seized the opportunity; it was the first wish her friend had expressed.

'Glory to God!' she shouted, overjoyed, forgetting there were others there. 'Can we come too, Fotis?'

'Oh, gladly! Gladly! Are you not afraid?'

They were not.

A trip to Aegina… a trip to Aegina with him, thought Anna, and her eyes lit up.

How had she not thought of this until today? How had she not thought of this way, among everything that she had tried, to drag him away from his night-mares? The island of their childhood was opposite them, and they saw it every day.

Overjoyed, her eyes aglow, Anna embraced Vaso: 'When the weather improves!'

'Yes, when the weather improves.'

CHAPTER THREE

Past

During the Great War, the three refugee families had lived in the same house on Aegina: the Venises, Aunt Maria with Angelos, and Aunt Sophia with her old father and Andreas. Andreas' younger sister Artemis was still around then, too.

'Do you remember Artemis, Anna?' Andreas asked, sitting next to her on the beach of Anavyssos.

She did not. She wanted to remember her, she really did, as she saw him for the first time showing an interest.

'What a rogue she was!' said Andreas. 'And she was always hungry back then, on Aegina…'

'But I remember, we were all hungry then.'

During those years, Dimitris Venis had found himself in a foreign environment where he had to struggle to survive. He realised he did not have the strength necessary for that sort of struggle—he was not made for it—and he lapsed into lethargy. He studied the Minoan era and cancer. He had long said his study was nearing completion, and then he would save humanity from the terrible disease. Later he spoke less on the subject. And then the Corsican came and cancer fell by the wayside.

'If there were no great men, perhaps you would make yourself useful,' Irini said bitterly to him.

Aunt Maria knitted socks all day long so that Angelos could go to school. From dawn, before anyone in the house had woken up, you could hear the wheel of her machine. She was perhaps the most pitiful of them all, for she had no one to support her, but she rarely wept in front of the others.

'Come on, Aunt Maria,' Artemis would say. 'Stop working now.'

Aunt Maria never wanted to let down the girl, whom she loved very much. She would comfort her during the blockade when she was hungry, when there was not enough bread.

'Come on, Artemis,' she would say in turn, 'get some rest now.'

And Artemis, as she really was a rogue and ran over the rocks all day, always fell asleep easily. That was why she dreamed more than the other children: more than Anna, Andreas and Angelos. 'You'll never guess what I dreamed last night!' she would say. And she told them. Her dreams were almost always the same: a hill or a forest, big and strange trees, colourful birds. That was where the bright house was, in which Artemis found herself one night. The sun was pouring in through great windows. In the middle a table was laid. What a wonderful spread there was! Too much to tell! With the sun shining onto it, she was afraid to touch the things, as if they were sacred beings. In her dream Artemis wore a light blue blouse with gold buttons, and she simply gazed at everything.

'Well, what happened next?' the other children asked.

'Nothing,' she said. 'That was it.'

'And you didn't even eat in your dream?' they joked.

'You should have been there. We'd see if you would have dared!' she replied.

Yes, she meant to tell them that they could not know what such a fear was like.

At other times Artemis would sit for hours leaning on the wooden fence that separated the courtyard of their house from the neighbouring mansion. A nobleman lived there, a man of independent means and inherited wealth. He had studied agriculture in England and did nothing but read books and grow chrysanthemums. Artemis loved bright colours. She would gaze at the flowers that grew up above the fence, listening to the music coming from the great house. The daughter of the house played the piano for two hours every day. Artemis forgot herself in the harmony of this other world beyond the fence. The girl who played was ugly, but she was very good. She was called Elizabeth. Often when Artemis was daydreaming on the fence, Elizabeth would send for her to be brought in. She would keep her a while and give her sweets. That made Artemis very happy.

'Mother, you should see what her hands feel like!' she said to Aunt Sophia when she returned.

That was what perplexed her most: how could human hands be so soft and untroubled? Her measure was the hands of her mother, who worked in various houses, or those of Aunt Maria, who turned the wheel of a machine from dawn.

In 1918 they dug up the bones of Andreas' and Artemis' grandmother, who had died in Aegina at the start of the war. That grandmother was one of the most goodly beings that God had deigned to send to earth. Their grandfather, who was still alive, took the bones to their house and stored them on the large shelf next to the icon of Archangel Michael.

Aunt Sophia was terribly afraid.

'Father, that won't do!' she said. 'It's bad for the bones to be in the house.'

But he was a simple, just, God-fearing man, and he would not be moved from his opinion.

'They will stay there,' he said, for he was afraid that they would be lost otherwise. 'We need to take them back to the East,' he added, by way of explanation. 'The war will be over shortly.'

When his daughter, Aunt Sophia, persisted, he said angrily, 'Aren't you ashamed to be afraid of your own mother? She's a saint now.'

Artemis' grandfather could stay for hours alone with the bones. The family had put him in a small room with them. Nothing scared him. Often, when he was standing and praying before the icons and the bones, in the dark, he spoke to the dead woman: 'Nearly there!' he encouraged her. 'A little longer and you'll be able to rest, Despina.'

If there happened to be good news from the war, victories of the Allies, he told her in the evening, 'We'll be home very soon!'

At other times he comforted her. She must not think he was going to delay in coming to her.

'I'll be coming soon,' he said. 'I'll just take you across the sea first, so you can rest.'

It was a reconciliation with death: a simple, solemn relationship. At night the children never went into that room, they were so afraid—Artemis the most. If her grandfather summoned her in the evening to see her —and he often did, since he was very fond of her— she would reply from outside the door, 'Don't call me, Grandpa. I'm afraid...'

Yes, she was afraid of death. And yet she was the first of all of them to go. She was laid to rest in the summer of 1918, just before the end of the war.

. . . .

The air was clear. In the serene distance Aegina was riding at anchor.

'Can you picture where the town is?' Andreas said to Anna, his eyes fixed on the island.

'On the right,' she said. 'Behind the headland.'

A cloud hung still above the island.

'To the right of the cloud,' said Anna. 'There! Why do you ask?'

'No reason.'

Then: 'How strange... that he should remember Artemis at a time like that...'

Anna looked at him uneasily.

'Who are you talking about?'

'Angelos.'

Back in the East, they had spent one night of their tortuous march in a village in the middle of the forest. It smelled of pines. They had been put in a stable. Angelos' eyes had lit up in the dark. 'Is something on your mind?' Andreas asked him. 'Me? No. I just remembered...' 'What?' 'The grave of the pine marten...' He was talking about a pine marten he had shamelessly killed in the fields of Aegina. Artemis had made a great fuss. She cried like a baby and buried the pine marten under a pear tree.

'You were talking about Angelos?' Anna asked.

'Yes, I was.'

Her heart beat hard. She felt that there lay his open wound.

'Did you suffer a lot?' she asked with deep emotion.

'Yes, Anna. We did.'

She pleaded fervently, her eyes moist, 'Come on, tell me. Talk to me. Unburden yourself. Talk to me.'

He withdrew abruptly, like a defensive animal.

'I have nothing to say.'

'No! No!' she persisted, and her eyes beseeched him. 'Tell me, tell me everything. It will do you good. Is he alive?'

She stroked his hands gently, to break down his resistance, to make him feel a voice, a friend in the wilderness, someone to lighten his burden.

'Is he alive?' she said again, more insistently.

Unable to resist anymore, he finally let his need for deliverance carry him away.

'No,' he said, and his eyes flooded with tears.

That evening, Anna did not let him go to Aunt Maria. They stayed on the ground floor, talking. The parents were out, and the two of them were alone.

'You'll see, Andreas. It will do you good to speak to me,' Anna said, arranging the lamp so as to hide her face and teary eyes.

From her room, they heard Aunt Maria talking to herself. They could not make out what she was saying. But her voice mingled with their memories of her lost son, and it was as though she was trying to make that other, silent voice last longer. And the sky outside, and the stars rising, and the sea, and all the harmony of the world tried to hold that voice too.

CHAPTER FOUR

Serenity

Day by day the weather improved. There were a few clouds in the sky, but they would disappear. Spring had come. Barba Kosmas, Vaso's father, sat in front of Fotis' shack with his eyes turned towards the hills of Anavyssos, his back to the sea.[9] Its roaring had died down, the wind had eased, and Barba Kosmas was calmer. When he first came to this coastal shack with his daughter after her marriage to Fotis, he had also been consumed with fear of the sea.

'How far does it stretch?' he asked Salia Balia, a retired Phocian skipper.

'Oooh!' he replied proudly. 'Just about to the end of the world.'

'And does this racket never stop?'

'Never!'

---

[9] 'Barba' is an affectionate term for an older male member of the community. It is prefixed to a given name.

He found the ceaseless movement incomprehensible. It shook his life, a life that had been spent in the solidity of great masses. Could he come to terms with it so late?

'My God,' he said to himself at night. 'Everything seems to be moving here. Like the water…'

Now that the weather was improving, Barba Kosmas started walking up the nearby hill. He would fill a sack with clean, sandless earth, put it on his shoulders and bring it to their shack. He was going to plant a plane tree, he said, at the door of the shack.

'A plane tree?' asked his son-in-law, Fotis. 'Do you think a plane tree could ever grow so close to the sea?'

'Why, do you think the salt water will bother it?'

'Of course it will. Here there's sea in the wind, too!'

Well, if that's so, Barba Kosmas will plant a poplar and be shaded by a tree of his country. You can become familiar with the shade of one tree, but not necessarily with the shade of another.

In his comings and goings to the hill, which was above Doctor Venis' rose garden, the two sometimes met and chatted. When the doctor found out that Barba Kosmas wanted earth, he smiled in his gentle way.

'You want to bring your homeland here to the sea, eh?'

Barba Kosmas, who had not realised that before, but now saw it clearly, replied, 'You do what you can.'

'Yes, you do what you can.'

He felt a sense of awe before the doctor, an awe towards his sacred vocation. For that reason he spoke little to him. On the other hand, he was freer and more familiar with the other old man, the retired skipper Salia Balia. Their age linked them, as did the years that had passed, and the approach of their shared end. People understand each other at the beginning and the end.

'Well, old countryman!' the Phocian would say to him, as they sat in the evenings on Barba Kosmas' straw mat outside Fotis' shack, in front of the pile of earth for the plane tree. 'Today's gone, too.'

'Yes, it's gone,' said Barba Kosmas.

'Did you hear any news?'

'No. You?'

'Nothing.'

Every day they waited. There was peace, but the papers signed by the powers decreed that they would not return to their homeland: the populations had been exchanged. Still, they waited.

'There's no way we're staying here,' said Barba Kosmas. 'They're swapping us around like animals! There's no way, I say, that we're dying here!'

The other, however, the old Phocian, had lived through another persecution, that of the Eastern Christians during the Great War. He had suffered. He was wiser.

'We'll die here, Kosmas. Believe me. We won't tread our earth again. Believe me.'

He listened, looking at the earth he had piled up handful by handful. A great tree will grow. If it's not a plane or an oak, it will be a poplar. Its trunk, he imagines, will rise above the walls of the shack and its branches will cover the roof with their shade. The wind will blow and all the leaves will play. They will play and spread. They will mingle with other leaves, then with others, until the trunks become entangled, struggle with each other for space: a forest of trunks and leaves, age-old trees and waters of the earth. The forest covers the salty sea and paces out beyond the waves, to the East.

'Are you still thinking about the plane tree?' asked the skipper.

He paused and then said softly, without waiting for an answer, 'It won't grow, Kosmas.'

'It won't,' he agreed sadly. 'Nor will we. But our children...'

A crowd of children were playing in front of them on the beach. Among them was Vaso's son, whom she had brought from the East. The children were playing with toy boats made of pinewood. They were pulling them with string, straining themselves to make their boat sink the others. Suddenly there was a scream. Vaso's child, who came from the border of Iran, withdrew in fright. The others, the little sea-children, had sunk his boat and he began to wail.

'He'll learn, don't worry,' said the skipper to Kosmas. 'Tomorrow they won't sink him. Do you even know

what it means to make a boat from pine? Your grand-
son made his own.'

Vaso's child came towards them in tears. His boat
was dripping salt water like his weeping eyes. Kosmas
took him in his arms and patted him.

'You'll learn,' he said. 'Don't cry.'

Looking at the boy, he tried to connect his features
with those of his father, whom the boy never knew.
The same year that Vaso married for the first time, the
government recruiters came, rounded up those who
could lift a rifle and took them to the lands of the setting sun. They took Vaso's husband too.

At some point they had news of him from
wounded men coming back from the fighting—some
from Arabia, others from the Dardanelles. Then nothing. Not a squeak. The second year of war came. Vaso's
boy had now been born. Then, one morning, the recruiters appeared again, rounding up the young men
who had grown up over the past year.

Again news came from the west, and again there
was silence. And then the recruiters came again, and
again. Now they sang a sad tune:

'The Dardanelles are too narrow for passing
And their murky waters are too bloody for drinking.'

Nothing was heard again about the boy's father, who
had been taken to the straits that the recruiters sang of.

Andreas went to the woods to gather pine cones for his mother.

'At least I can help you with the fire,' he said with shame, even though she had no complaint with him at all.

He lay down under a tree. The resin smelled strong. All the world's serenity could be found under that pine tree.

'Hullo!' said Anna, emerging from the narrow path. 'I followed you here.'

He looked at her tenderly. But it was clear that even at this moment he had more on his mind than her.

'You don't seem well again these last days,' said Anna. 'What's wrong?'

He could not tell her of the inertia that was gradually polluting his veins, nor of the sudden change in the rhythm of his life since he had arrived. It was a sinister, supicious serenity—how could he tell her of the black cloud that hovered over him? If only he could at least consolidate one thought—exhaust it, make it flesh, with definite lines! But everything tires him, nothing leads anywhere, and his nerves, muscles and blood are destroyed. Gradually, the most solid matter—memories from the past—weakens, transformed into something dark and shapeless. That weakening was also a power. What if that disappeared, too? The night is often desolate with nightmares. What would it be without Anna? She was the only certainty remaining in this fearful, empty place.

And Anna was still very young. She could smell the enemy fighting her in the dark, but she did not know how, or if, she could strike it.

'What's wrong?' she asked him again.

'Nothing, Anna.'

They got up and gathered pine cones.

'Let's go to see my father,' said Anna, on their descent from the forest.

The rose garden was on their way. The plants had taken root. Dimitris Venis now believed they would grow. But it was all in the hands of the god of the place. Only of the god? Oh, how much human effort is spent on just one root!

Dimitris called them over with his goodly smile, his small gestures, his gentle voice: 'Come and look!'

A dung beetle was patiently driving a small lump of manure to its nest. It became tired, stopped, hit an obstacle, the lump snagged on a stone, the dung beetle stoically rocked its black being onto one side, then the other. The enemy was brushed aside and the slow march began again.

'He's got a purpose,' said Dimitris with a smile.

Then, more seriously, he said to Andreas, 'That is everything. All wisdom.'

They sat to watch evening falling over the sea.

Beyond the Saronic Gulf, beyond the Aegean, a small, silver fish suddenly sees a still light on the seabed. It is a strange, watery light, twitching in the eyes of the whale that will enclose in its dark depths anything that comes towards it. The silver fish knows that this is its end. Yet it is the end that it pursued and that all the silver fish before it have found.

'May I ask you,' said Dimitris to Andreas, 'about your life?'

Anna had gone some distance away, down to the beach below the rose garden. The two of them were alone.

'Yes, Doctor.'

He perceived the affection in the good man's eyes, understood the emotions with which he followed at young Anna's side.

'What do you plan to do now in your life?' Dimitris said. 'Have you decided?'

'No, Mr Venis. I don't know what to do here.'

And then, agitated, his voice animated, he pleaded, 'Won't you help me? Every morning I wake up so anxious...'

'Yes, child, I understand,' Venis said softly. 'But I will talk to you as an old man, not as a doctor. Do you see what I have done here since we came?'

'Yes, Mr Venis, I see. You're making an effort...'

He hesitated, as if not wanting to give a clear answer.

'Speak! Speak clearly!' the doctor encouraged him.

'I think... I think... that you are chasing fantasies,' the young man said, his eyes smiling. 'These roses...'

Dimitris' kindly eyes now fixed on him.

'No, not only that,' he said gently. 'It's not only for the roses themselves...'

After a while he said, 'For serenity.'

That is the purpose. The final purpose. That is why he torments his body.

'Still, I believe...' he murmured. 'And if that is fantasy...'

Serenity! In the calm, the tumult, in the water that relaxes as it forms a cloud, in the clouds that clash during the storm and try to cast out their water and find peace, in the passions of people who struggle and fight, in the people who suffer because they were not destined to do anything, in the bodies that struggle for love, in the stars that tumble down at night, in the earth that turns, in dreams and deeds, in everything the search for a lost balance, a ceaseless recomposition.

'Yes, I torment my body, and I believe,' Dimitris Venis said.

'Oh! How I have tormented my body too.'

'Yet you did not do it of your own accord. There is a difference.'

The sun was setting over the mountains of Aegina.

'You have the whole universe open before you,' said Dimitris. 'You must look for its furthest corner. My life is now ending, but I don't let myself not believe, not try,' he added.

'This small, enclosed place doesn't help,' said the young man. 'At least, if I were in a city...'

'You would disappear more easily there,' said Dimitris. 'Place is here!' and he touched his forehead with his finger.

'Yes.'

'You were put in rags when you were just children,' Dimitris said. 'That did not happen to us. Perhaps that is the reason we can now understand each other—you at one end of life, us at the other.'

Anna came with a handful of pebbles from the beach.

'What are you talking about?' she asked them, seeing how serious they looked.

'About the joy of the world.'

'So it seems, from your faces,' she said with a smile.

Then, observing the approaching dusk: 'We need to go, Father. It's chilly... Oh look, there's Mother!' she said, looking towards the end of the mole just beyond the shacks.

Irini Venis was walking alone along the coast path leading to the rocks. She was wrapped in the red light of the spring evening, as if in a dream. She was all alone: her and the red light.

We have the same end in mind, thought Dimitris, but our paths did not meet.

No one ventured to call her. And she did not turn around to look towards the rose garden. She kept walking, looking at the Saronic Gulf, then disappeared behind the rocks.

'Let's go back,' said Dimitris.

'It's easy to catch a cold at this time of year,' said Anna.

'Mother, I have some news to announce!' Anna said at the dinner table, a strange glow in her eyes.

'News?' said Irini. 'Really, news?'

'Really! News, Mother!'

She waited for a moment. Unconsciously, involuntarily, she relished the suspense.

'Father's roses seem to be growing,' she said at last, and the glow remained in her eyes. 'Yes, it was absolutely clear!'

Irini raised her eyes and turned them slowly from her daughter's face to those of the others. Dimitris looked at her with a gentle, assured smile, illuminated by his blue eyes: so assured, like a knife fixed over her, ready to fall. Her older sister, Aunt Maria, had lowered her head and was leaning slightly to one side, absorbed in herself, digging in her memory, in her hands, in her blood, for the voice from the past, the voice from the future that awaits her. *She can wait her whole life.* And the girl, little Anna… Oh, Anna could only wait. She had learned nothing else yet.

Irini Venis realised that she alone remained a stranger, with nothing to wait for or believe in, though this human landscape had been watered with the same blood that ran in her veins.

She jumped up violently.

'I tell you, the roses will not grow!' she cried, fixing her eyes on her husband. 'I tell you they will not grow!'

But he was overcome by that merciless power that rejoices in the defeat of others. He said, 'They will.' His voice was soft and formal. 'You'll see, Irini. They will grow!'

'I told you it's impossible!' shouted Irini, now furious. 'You'll see that they won't grow! You'll see!'

And, unable to endure any more, she fled into the night.

. . . .

'Go to your mother, Anna,' Aunt Maria said later. 'She is more alone than anyone.'

'Father is alone too,' said Anna stubbornly. 'Why does she have to take away the joy he gains from his hopes?'

'Go to your mother, child,' Aunt Maria said again, calmly. 'Your father is not alone.'

CHAPTER FIVE

Trip to Aegina

Fotis looked at the sky, consulting the clouds.

'We will set off at dawn,' he said.

He sent Zabeta to tell Anna to come if they wished. Whatever happened, the trip to Aegina would take place tomorrow. 'We have no jugs here. A boatful will sell like hot cakes.' Thus he assigned the purpose of the trip.

'We'll get to Aegina in four hours. I'll stay another four. That's eight. The return can last as long as it needs.'

Anna ran off happily to tell Andreas.

'Will Vaso come too?' she asked Fotis.

'Of course she will. She needs to break her bile.'

'Will the boat take all four of us?'

'Of course!' he said proudly. 'There'll be another, too.'

She took umbrage at this.

'Who?'

'The lad from the Dodecanese. Haritos.'

Yes, Anna had seen him. Everyone in the shacks knew each other, and their stories were written on their faces. Every new face was a new page that the others had to read.

Haritos had disembarked one day from a boat that had come to load up with salt for the Dodecanese. The boat loaded and left, but he stayed to make his fortune in the salt pans. He looked for work persistently, but there was none. He wandered for days and days through the villages and shacks. Then, one day, he stopped in front of Fotis' windmill. He was impressed.

'If you have any work for me, all I ask is my upkeep. I'm quite handy on a boat or on the land.'

'Very well,' Fotis said, flattered to have been asked for work, as happened to the wealthy. 'When the weather improves, there might be work on the boat and the land. I'll call for you.'

He gave him food.

'Why did you stay here?' he asked, not curious about anything else in his life.

'I couldn't live there,' he said, pointing towards the islands in the south. 'They were after me.'

He explained that on the islands he had worked with a band of sailors who lived by secretly fishing in the waters of the mainland opposite. They staked everything on their boats and nets, for fishing was strictly prohibited in those border waters. One day a Turkish pursuit vessel caught them. Their livelihoods were destroyed. They took their boats, put them in prison and tore up their nets, then sent them back to the island.

Haritos embarked on a boat heading for Cretan waters, which left him in Sitia. There he learned that one of his brothers, lost since the years of the Great War, was living in Piraeus. He found a way to embark for the great port, where he suffered for several months, going hungry and looking for his brother. In desperation he boarded a boat that would return to the Dodecanese after loading up with salt from the pans at Anavyssos. He disembarked, saw the land was gentle and stayed, fearing to go on.

The Great Bear was low in the sky when Fotis went to wake Haritos.

'Come on!'

He gave him two small, empty sacks.

They made for the salt pans. Fotis had not told anyone of his plans: he did not want their opinion. Haritos followed close behind in silence, asking nothing.

The white pyramids of salt stood out clearly before them.

'Quiet!' Fotis said. 'They mustn't hear us. We'll fill the sacks in secret.'

'Well, the sea's barren,' he had said to himself, when he was thinking of stealing salt. 'We need to live, too,' and he smiled at his plan. The salt cost him nothing, and he would go to Aegina to turn it into valuable jugs.

The morning star had risen over the hills of Anavyssos when the fishing boat left the bay. Those planks of wood from the Romanian forests, brought on the Danube, now carried across the sea some salt and five people so utterly alone that none of them even suspected their loneliness.

'Where do you come from?' Vaso had asked the stranger who arrived in her father's shack on the borders of Iran, that night of her childhood. 'From the sea,' he had answered. 'Is that some kind of golden sky?' 'No, it's salt water!'

'This place has no jugs'—thus Fotis, her husband, had assigned the purpose of their journey.

He was turning this purpose over in his mind, when his eyes fell on Vaso's shadowy body in the bow of the boat.

'What are you thinking about?' he asked her, guessing her fear as he looked at that indefinable mass of silent flesh and bones.

'Nothing,' said Vaso. 'I am wondering if Zabeta will milk the goat in the evening if we're late.'

The morning dew penetrated their bones, stirring the blood. A fresh vigour oozed into their marrow, fibres and nerves.

I need to start working. I need to get my teeth into something, Andreas thought, moved by this awakening. It'll do me good.

Loneliness seeped into Anna's heart, the same solitude that had possessed the researchers who wrote those books of her father's. During the war, they had been young children on the island where the boat was taking them. In the olive grove, under a tree, Andreas had kissed her and asked, 'When I grow up, will you come with me to the ocean?' 'Only if you become a captain,' she had replied, because she had no fondness for cowards, but only wanted the strong. 'Then I will become a captain!' he said. And Anna expected a strong captain to come from the East and take her in his arms.

Only the fifth passenger, the lad from the Dodecanese, was a blank page. No one had written it, nor even turned to it. Fotis was on the tiller. The boy had nothing to do now. He was sitting in the prow with his bare legs hunched and crossed, so as not to take up too much space.

The morning star faded. The lines of the hills began to be written clearly, far off, as in a dream. Anna's eye fell on the boy, who was himself taking shape in the dawn light. He was very young, short and thin, with strong arms. It was obvious that considerable force was hidden under his skin. He had a low forehead and his hair was wild, thick and dark.

'Aren't you going to say anything to him?' Anna whispered to Andreas.

Andreas looked back, uncomprehending. But she knew about loneliness, and turned towards the prow: 'Come down here with us.'

Taken aback, Haritos turned towards her voice.

'Me?'

'Yes, come down here.'

He did not dare to object, but got up hesitantly and sat beside them.

'Are you happy in our country?' Anna said.

'Yes. Very.'

'Oh, he's a good and capable worker,' shouted Fotis from the tiller. 'I have no complaint with him.'

'Do you have a father?' Anna asked.

No, he did not. His father had left to go hunting one day and did not return.

'Where was that? On the islands?'

'No, in the East. Only there can a person disappear like that. There are bears and fearful mountains.'

'But are you not from the Dodecanese?'

No, he was born in the East. Amid the persecutions of Christians they had fled to the islands. Then, when the war finished, his family returned. With the disaster of 1922, however, they went back to the islands. There were four brothers. Two of them were killed in the war, the third disappeared, and Haritos searched for him, but without success. Their mother lived on the islands.

'Which place do you remember best?' Anna asked.

This interrogation started to bother him, for he was a closed person and not used to others caring about these insignificant facts of his life.

'I don't know,' he said, and looked at the sea.

They were now some way from the shore, and there were strong waves in the gulf. One came and struck the front of the boat, but before Fotis managed to luff away, another came powerfully, filling the boat with foam and water.

'Oh!' cried Vaso, terrified, 'Holy Mother of God!'

'Oh!' Anna cried too, and in a move to protect herself fell onto Andreas' chest.

There was a momentary commotion. Fotis lost his cool and lashed out at Vaso. 'Why are you wailing like a bloodhound?' he shouted. 'Be quiet!'

She folded her arms, gathered her fear in her eyes and fell silent.

'Don't be scared,' Andreas said gently, to Anna, who was still leaning on him, and stroked her head.

Then the waves in the gulf vanished, the sea became calm, and the girl remained peacefully on the chest of the man whose spirit was awakening.

'Don't be scared,' he said, and stroked her.

It was honest wood and it carried the five bodies towards their fate.

'Nothing has changed! Nothing has changed! Do you remember it, Andreas?' Anna kept saying, as they entered the harbour of Aegina.

Joy shone on her face.

'Shall we go to all our old places?'

'We shall,' he said, swept up by her joy.

'To the olive grove too?' she asked, looking at him to see if he remembered.

Of course he did!

'Yes, yes, to the olive grove!'

When they moored, they abandoned the others and made for the old house in which they had spent the four years of their childhood during the Great War.

Nothing had changed. Only the road seemed narrower. Roads do seem narrower, as the years go by. In the low house with the great courtyard, trees they had planted back then had grown tall.

They entered the courtyard and halted at once with emotion, as if a new face of the world had appeared before them, unknown and powerful.

'Look at that wall!' Andreas said under his breath.

There was a shack opposite the house. Angelos had written his name large on the wall in whitewash: *Angelos*. He was there no more, yet the letters in whitewash remained.

A woman, sitting in the house, came to the door.

'Are you looking for something?' she asked, seeing them staring.

'No, thank you,' Andreas said. 'I am looking at the letters on the wall.'

The woman looked at him inquisitively. 'Do you know the person who wrote them?'

'No, I don't.'

Then, moved by a sudden thought, and from a feeling of affection, he asked, 'Did you, by chance, hear anything about him?'

'How could I? It was war. People came and went.'

She told them she was from Adana. They came here in 1922.

'Can we have a look inside?' Andreas asked.

'Oh, gladly!' she said eagerly, more and more surprised.

The rooms were even more modest and bleak than when they had lived there. The plaster had completely crumbled and the wooden framework of the walls stood out like bones. Here, near the window, Aunt Maria had set up her machine and knitted socks all day. Andreas and Angelos had found work in the bakery of Barba Stathis. In the morning they went to school and in the evening to the bakery. The work was not very hard. But when a child is working, how hard everything is! They carried water and filled the great earthenware jar. They washed the troughs. They brought wood. Sometimes they even kneaded bread. At first they were given a small loaf for four or five hours' work. That bread was a great help to their families, especially in the era of the blockade of Greece, when it was rationed.

When Andreas and Angelos returned home late, Artemis, Anna and the others were fast asleep. Only the boys' mothers stayed awake, waiting for them. Aunt Maria could not work late on her machine, as it made a great racket, so she would read the Scriptures quietly. The two women were relaxed then, and sometimes, when their children returned, they found them asleep over the open book. They did not wake them, but merely dimmed the lamp and nestled under the covers. When the mothers woke up and saw their children had come back and were asleep, they went to rest too. Most often, however, the children found them awake, waiting. They opened the gate softly and heard Aunt Maria's voice whispering as she read. When they noticed the children, they stood up at once. 'Ah, you're back,' Aunt Maria said with relief. She looked at Angelos inquisitively, uneasily. 'Are you very tired?' she asked him. He set the wrapped piece of bread in her hands—the fruit of his night's toil. 'It does not tire me, Mother,' he said. 'But why are you waiting up?' On that subject, they would not hear a word. They would wait up. And when one day Angelos insisted on asking his mother why she did this, since she was not helping him in any way by doing so, she did not know how to respond. Once only she told him that if she was sleeping while he was out, she would be afraid he was in danger. She stayed up to guard him against the dark enemy.

. . . .

'Up there was once a shelf,' Andreas said to the woman from Adana.

'How do you know?' she asked in surprise.

'We had icons there.'

'Oh, you lived here, then?'

'Yes, we did.'

'I see.'

The chest with the grandmother's remains had been on that shelf. Artemis' presence was all around them.

Andreas then said to the woman from Adana, 'Of course, you must always hear music from next door.'

'Do you mean the daughter of the learned man?'

'Yes, Elizabeth.'

'Ah! She left last year. They say she has gone far away. Now the house is very quiet.'

During the Great War, in 1916, the neighbouring house had hosted a passing Australian air officer. The good houses used to give this kind of hospitality during the war. In the spring of 1916, the violets and geraniums of the nobleman had come out early and the earth smelled sweet. 'Elizabeth, play me a song about spring,' the foreigner had implored. They were alone in the room, they and the night that had fallen over the gulf. How far away the war was! 'I will play you a song about spring.' Later the Australian left for the Western Front. Years passed and peace arrived. One day the Australian appeared on the island from his distant land.

'I have come, Elizabeth, to take you with me. Will you come?'

The song, along with the Greek spring, had travelled with him.

'I will,' she responded.

And she followed him beyond the ocean.

'Now?' Anna said to Andreas as they were leaving the house. 'Now let's go to the olives.'

Both of them were shaken by their visit to the old house, but he seemed the more moved. Anna wanted to bring him out of the gloomy mood.

'I have no past,' she had said one day, seeing him withdrawn and in thought. 'Now my life is beginning.'

'I cannot stand this anymore,' he remarked sadly.

'Shall we go to the olive grove?' Anna asked again, believing only in the past that fertilises the future.

'We shall, Anna. But first I want to see Barba Stathis.'

'He might have died,' said the young woman, insisting they go to the olives.

'No, I want to see him. I owe him a lot.'

It was true: he owed him a lot.

The bakery was on the edge of the small town. Houses, most of them ramshackle, were scattered thinly around it. From the great window of the bakery, when Andreas and Angelos worked there, they could see the sea and the little harbour. There was an olive tree at the bakery door.

Back then in the bakery worked Barba Stathis, an unmarried daughter of his—Virginia—and the two lads, Andreas and Angelos. When they went for water at the fountain, they were often late in returning, especially when they passed the gypsies with the bears. The two of them would stare at the heavily chained beasts that were made to dance. At other times, at night, they would fall asleep on the counter of the bakery. Then Barba Stathis, who worked like a dog, would shout, 'You rascals! Lazy slugs! You think that's how bread is made? I'll do for you!'

He shouted viciously and swore so much he raised the roof. The boys cowered, and Virginia too, but they were used to it and were not afraid. They knew he would never hit them. They waited a while for him to calm down.

'When I was your age, I worked with Vergas,' he said, starting to calm down.

When they heard him talking about his youth, they knew the storm had passed. Then they waited for him to tell stories from his turbulent life. He painted a vivid picture, taking from his memories the firm lines that create character or drama and expressing them with the simplicity of the common speech. Vergas seemed to have been a fearsome smuggler and captain who had worked on the islands of the archipelago and on the mainland opposite. One of his comrades dishonourably betrayed him to the officials, who tied up the smuggler and did away with him off a remote island east of Lesbos. His comrades retrieved the corpse, took it to Ayvali and buried it. When they had left for the island, they took their captain's young son with them. The traitor, who was on the boat, feigned ignorance. The others said nothing, so he would not suspect anything. One day, when a great storm was blowing, they came to the remote island. As they were eating, the young lad, Vergas' son, stood up. 'You weren't worthy of eating bread with my father,' he said to the traitor. 'And yet you destroyed him.'

He drew the knife they had given him and, before the startled man could protect himself, the boy stabbed him twice in the shoulder. But his hand was trembling. The others around him looked at the scene in silence, motionless, letting the boy exact his debt alone. Then, as the traitor tried to get up, he knocked him down with another stab of the knife. Barba Stathis, still very young, stood up, pinned the man on his back and knelt on his chest. He grabbed the hand of Vergas' kneeling son, brought it over the heart and helped him plunge it in with force.

'Learn how to strike straight,' he said.

Barba Stathis told such stories at night in his bakery. And the children—Andreas, Angelos and Virginia—were plunged into the theatre of the old world, which played with blood and death.

'What do you understand from that world, though?' said Barba Stathis. 'Why am I telling you this?'

'Why?' answered the boys. 'Ask us who we want to be like when we grow up!'

'Well, who?'

Before they answered, however, he said with a smile, 'I know.' Indeed he knew how much they wanted to resemble that worthy, courageous man.

In turn, he was very fond of them. He used to receive letters occasionally from his sons, who were at the front. At first they said they would be back very soon. But the war came to an end and time passed. Barba Stathis' hair turned whiter every day. Work tired him out.

'When will they come to relieve me?' he said.

He hardly ever left the bakery. In the afternoons, when the weather was good, he went out and sat under the olive tree at the door. That was now all his movement in the endless world. The children called it 'the journey.' Sometimes the journey would lengthen, as Barba Stathis forgot himself under the tree for a long while. He rolled a cigarette and sat there smoking, looking at the sea. But it was the birds he noticed most. He who had lived such a tough and bloody life had an incomprehensible tenderness for birds. He could not tell them apart, and he never said their names. He just watched them pass.

'A group of them went by!' he said when he returned to the bakery, as if bringing some great news. 'Five of them. They were heading south.'

'What do you think they were, Barba Stathis?' Andreas and Angelos asked, knowing he could not tell them. 'What could they be?'

'What comes of knowing that?' he would say. 'Just watching them fly is enough, I say.'

'But it's not enough, Barba Stathis. People need to know what bird it is, to know whether to shoot it or not.'

'Damn the moment they learn!' cursed Barba Stathis. 'Why should the animals of the earth die simply for our food? Let the goodly things fly and be happy.'

The children then remembered their morning zoology lesson: learning species, groups, habitats… And finally, every time, what each animal or bird gives, how it is useful to man. Everything they studied, the whole approach to the world, was directed at this lesson: what use each animal is to man. Later they would understand why the children with imagination were selfish and tough.

'What animals, what birds, Barba Stathis!' Angelos said. 'Everything was made for man. That's what the books say. Are they lying?'

When the discussion reached that point, the old baker became tired. He was simple, unlettered, and had great respect for books. But still he did not want to let the matter go. One day, after apparently a great deal of thought, he said, 'Listen here: what else in the world flies, other than birds?'

'What else, Barba Stathis? Only birds.'

'Well, think about it. The birds… and the angels! Therefore they are sacred. Birds and angels…'

'But sandflies and bats also fly, Barba Stathis,' the children said mischievously. 'And stink bugs…'

He fumed and stamped his foot.

'Listen to me, you rogues! Birds and angels…'

He had lived a tough life, working for years as a smuggler and sticking by the young son of his leader as he was exacting his debt. When he had reached his end, watching the birds going past, he was brought news that his first son would not return from the front.

He put on a black shirt. And the women from the hill keened in the courtyard of the bakery. They sat on the ground, making a circle around Virginia and staring at her as she pulled out her hair under the sun and dug her nails into her dark face, wailing and weeping. Then the chorus followed the leader.

Only Barba Stathis took no part in the libation. He neither spoke, nor shouted, nor cried. He abandoned the birds, too. He sat for hours in the shade of the olive tree and looked at the ground. The sea ebbed and flowed below, the birds came and went above, and he looked at nothing. Only the ground. The mystery had just begun: the deep bond that binds humans to the earth at the hour of their ordeal.

. . . .

'Shall we ask if he's alive?' Anna asked Andreas as they went up the hill. 'He might have died, and we would be going needlessly.'

'We'll see,' he said decisively. 'Come on, Anna.'

From afar they made out the low house of the bakery. An old man was sitting on the wall of the courtyard.

'That's him, that's him...' murmured Andreas, as they approached. 'Do you see?'

Shortly they were in front of him.

'Good day, Barba Stathis.'

The old man's eyes were lowered to the ground and he was still—leaning over, they understood, to search for that voice in the depths of his past.

'Welcome,' he said softly, before asking, 'Who are you?'

Andreas knelt on the ground to kiss his hand.

'It's me, Barba Stathis! Do you not recognise me?'

Then, with the young man on his knees, the old man raised his eyes for the first time, revealing that the light had left them.

'It's me, Barba Stathis! Andreas, who worked with Angelos in the war years. Remember?'

A brief moment passed. Then the old man fondly pulled him close.

'I didn't recognise your voice, child,' he said, his lips trembling. 'Now I can only recognise people by their voice. You seem to have grown up a lot.'

'It's been many years, Barba Stathis. Yes, I've grown up a lot.'

'What happened to you in the disaster?' he asked. 'Where have you come from?'

'From the East. The Turks kept me there.'

'Ah, they kept you, too…'

Another moment passed.

'My other son… Do you remember Pavlos?'

'Just about, Barba Stathis. Did he return?'

He lowered his voice.

'No. He did not return, either. We lost him.'

Ah, the second son, too.

'Is Virginia alive?'

She is indeed, working in a factory. She leaves in the morning and returns late in the evening. The bakery has closed now.

'We're the last ones left,' Barba Stathis said softly. 'My daughter and I…'

A moment passed.

'Where do you live?'

'Over there, on the other side of the sea. In Anavys-sos. I will come to see you again.'

'You're a good lad… I always said so… And your friend, what happened to him?'

No response.

'Angelos, I mean,' persisted Barba Stathis. 'What happened to him?'

Andreas replied brusquely, 'We lost him.'

'Ah, him too. The whole world was turned upside down. I only hear strange voices around me now. From Adana, from the Pontus, from the ends of the earth.'

'Yes, from the ends of the earth.'

'Nothing stayed in its place.'

How could he contain such turmoil at the end of his life? Once, birds passed above him and the man had sat and watched them go by. Were they still going by? His eyes could see no more, and their calls did not reach him. The birds must have changed their route over the sea.

Midday was approaching. The sun was hovering above Aegina, above the temple of Aphaia and the shoulders of the old man.

'Now I must go home,' Barba Stathis said. 'Come along too, won't you?'

But he paused, his ears pricked up. Anna had moved.

'Who is that with you?' he asked, fixing his closed eyes on Andreas.

'That's… my fiancée. Do you remember the daughter of Doctor Venis?'

'My dear! Come here,' said the old man, stretching his hands into empty space to find the girl. 'Why didn't you tell me all this time?'

He took Anna's hand, held it in his own and stroked it. Then he fumbled for Andreas' hand.

'Ah, your fiancée,' he said. 'She must have grown up a lot!'

Then: 'May you be very happy.'

The girl, surprised by the word 'fiancée', hearing it for the first time at that moment, did not know what to say and was moved to silence.

They tried to help him up and into his shack, but he resisted.

'There's no need, children. See, I have counted the steps now. I've learned them.'

He continued slowly but steadily to the shack. Inside it was austere. On a small table were the lamp and matches, and photographs of his two boys. Barba Stathis sat on the ground, leaning against the wall.

'Now I will wait for my daughter. She will come back early today. Will you wait to see her?'

No, it is late and they need to leave.

'My day is over, too,' the old baker said softly. 'In the afternoon it gets chilly and I don't go out. I get cold.'

They bid him goodbye and left his little hideout. How bright it was outside! How bright it is on Aegina!

CHAPTER SIX

Love

Andreas took Anna and pulled her forcefully, at a run, towards their beloved place outside the main town of Aegina. The heavy wave of misery and of the bitter past stirred unexpected, dormant strengths inside him. His hot blood and slumbering youth roused a new voice—a sense of existence, beyond the misfortunes of the world. He pulled the girl and she ran along, panting, beside him.

'Slow down, Andreas!' she shouted. 'I'm tired!'

'Come on! Come on!' he said, and sparks flew from his eyes. 'You can rest when we're there.'

Then, in his madness, he remembered something, and his eyes opened wider.

'Will it be running?'

'What are you talking about?'

'About the water. Our stream.'

There was a stream in the olive grove, where he used to go on Sundays and set up a net for the goldfinches. Anna often accompanied him there. Together they covered the stream with leaves, apart from where they had set up the net. Then Andreas hid behind the great olive tree, holding the string of the net in his hand. He would sit there for many hours, waiting for a bird to come and drink, and he would pull the string to catch it in his net. Anna could not stand such stillness. She climbed the nearby trees, shrieked, fell, got up again; life for her was not sitting and waiting. Andreas reprimanded her for chasing away the birds. '*I* am chasing them away?' she said. 'Listen to this greenfinch.' She made the call of a greenfinch and flapped her arms like wings. When she was tired she went to rest beside him. She lay on her back, breathed deeply and looked at the sky. Her breath gradually became calmer, until her eyes closed. They could stay like that for hours, in silence. Andreas' mind was always on the net. Yet, constantly watching the same spot, his eyes gradually clouded over and he started drifting off too. Then the sounds became clearer: the olive leaves whispering, a branch breaking, the whistling of a bird. The earth had become green and fragrant. If an insect moved, you could hear its steps. They stayed absorbed like that for many hours. The goldfinches came down to the water, on the stretched net, drank and left. No one was going to disturb them. One such summer's day, next to the stream, he had leant down and kissed her powerfully on the mouth.

'Let's hope that the stream is still running,' Andreas kept saying.

Arriving out of breath and with racing hearts, they leaned their heads over the low bank.

'Glory to God!'

Clear water was running beneath their young eyes.

'Nothing has changed...'

Then she repeated, with emotion, 'Nothing has changed.'

'There's the tree, Anna!'

They saw the gnarled trunk nearby.

Peace was thick around them. On the opposite bank a solitary chaffinch was singing. He pulled her to the old tree and they sat down. The girl leaned on her side at first, then lay down and sighed. She closed her eyes. Andreas turned towards her to say something. But he hesitated. Beneath his eyes, her chest stretched her thin blouse in a desperate attempt to spring out. After all their running, a strong rose colour had spread over her wheaten face. From her gently trembling, half-open lips, came the sacred invocation calling them to leave. It was an invitation to travel, beyond the seas, beyond their bitterness, beyond the past, beyond the rule of memory. As she had lain down, her skirt had risen above her knees and a small part of the wondrous young body was lit strangely by the sun—a particle of independent matter, young and alone, trying to begin its life on earth.

He leaned over her gingerly. 'If only you knew how much I love you, Anna.'

She did not open her eyes. Only her lips moved a fraction.

Then, on the instant, his hesitating hands flew at her waiting body.

He kissed her madly, clasped her with his troubled hands. All the strength of his body, silent for so many months, gushed out violently, dense, dark and tyrannical. The concentrated strength found refuge and escape at the tips of the fingers, the hands and muscles. The girl writhed under this primeval force with instinctive resistance. Two buttons on her blouse broke and the curves of her chest glowed in the sun. He thrust his hands into this open gate and closed his eyes. And the girl stopped resisting.

He grabbed her wildly, painfully, like an animal with its prey. And the leaves of the tree took their groans and scattered them over their bodies, like fragments of light.

When Fotis had sold his salt, he bought jugs with the proceeds and was satisfied.

'These will sell like hot cakes in Anavyssos! Excellent work!'

He went down to the harbour where Vaso was sitting on the mole next to the boat.

She stood up when she saw him. Fotis wanted to tell someone how well his work had gone, but his wife could not be that person.

'What have you been doing?' he asked merely.

She pointed to the sea and said meekly, 'Nothing. I was waiting for you.'

Fotis would like to ask her, now that the purpose of the journey had been accomplished, if she was pleased he had brought her to a new place. But he could not ask her that either. What of it, if she liked it or not? He simply raised his eyes to see where the sun was.

'We can set sail shortly,' he said. 'I see no reason to wait for nightfall.'

At that moment Haritos appeared, carrying the last load of jugs. He put them in the hold.

'Have you seen the others anywhere?' Fotis asked him. 'We'll need to go shortly.'

No, he had not.

Fotis smiled knowingly and his clever eyes danced.

'They lingered by the stream, eh? Go and find them!' he odered Haritos. 'It's just over that hillock.'

He pointed eastwards to the place.

'Tell them to come.'

Haritos made for the place the captain had indicated, to find them. He left the last houses behind and came to the bare earth. It smelled strongly, and beneath the hot stones the scorpions were waking. They know spring by its smell. The clouds will no longer cover the sky, it will only be blue light up in the roof of the world, and stars. When the moon comes out at night, the scorpions will wake one by one from their nests, immersed in hibernation and desire, and they will smell the air to see if the female has woken and left. If not, they will wait patiently. Then she will come out and sit on a hot stone, and one by one the males will pass before her, so she can choose the strongest. And when that is done, he will let her drag him to her nest. But first he will turn and look at the night and stars, knowing that he will not see them again. Then, obedient and happy, he will follow his destiny. All night he will enjoy his passion, violently and exhaustingly. And when he has worn himself out, the female will begin to eat her bridegroom slowly, regaining the strength she has lost. Then, when the sun shines on the morrow, she will rest happily. And when the coolness tells her the stars are out again in the roof of the sky, she will leave her nest to choose the next bridegroom, who will be waiting.

'Aren't you going swimming?' a noble girl of his island homeland had once tempted Haritos. She was not older than Anna, but her body was even more mature. 'No,' he responded, for when honourable sailors come of age and take the tiller in their hands, it is not right for them to play in the sea like children. 'Take me out in your boat. I will swim.' Haritos lowered his head to avoid the temptation. His temples pounded, his whole body trembled. He took her out. The girl jumped into the sea and swam off. Haritos remained fighting with the demon inside him, his blood boiling, when he heard her desperate voice. She had grown tired and was crying for help. He stripped off and jumped into the sea without thinking, instead of going towards her with his boat. He grabbed her just before she went completely under, and dragged her away, her young body dangling from his fingers in the water. He swam with one hand and with the other held her chest under his arm, clasping his hand onto the tight flesh. This was his first meeting with a woman's body.

'What is your name?' she asked when she came around.

He told her.

'Come home to see my father, for all your effort.'

But Haritos did not go. He did not know what was the price of his efforts.

'Are you happy that you came to our country?' Anna had asked him when they left in the morning. But Haritos saw her fingers searching for those of the boy, Andreas, who was beside her in the boat. And he knew that only when hands are incapable of moving, on a dangling body, are they not an enemy.

Why would they tarry in this desolate place? Haritos thought.

She must be in his arms. She might even be naked under a tree…

He continued gingerly, looking right and left. When he found the stream that Fotis had told him about, he hesitated a moment, not knowing if he should follow it up or down. He opted for the downwards path. He heard the chaffinch calling from the opposite bank. The sun was burning in the trees and on his face.

Suddenly he heard groans, and stopped behind a tree. Not far off, just a few metres away, Anna was writhing in her painful sacrifice. Haritos saw the light strangely binding her half-naked, virginal body to the earth. Sweat pricked his forehead, his eyes widened, his body trembled and his nails scratched the dry tree trunk until his fingers were bloodied.

He watched to the end.

He waited for quiet, for the groans to stop. The girl covered her nudity and the boy got up. Then Haritos emerged from the cover of the tree and headed towards them.

'The captain is waiting for you,' he said, looking at the ground. 'We're leaving.'

He turned to leave at once, but Andreas called him back.

'We're coming. Wait and we'll go together.'

On the return, Anna begged them to take a detour past the small bakery and their former home.

'But it's faster the other way,' said Andreas.

'No. I don't want to.'

They took a path that would lead them further to the west. Haritos walked just in front, his eyes lowered. Anna walked behind him, tired out, leaning on Andreas' arm. Her eyes were flooded with revelation, and her gaze fell instinctively on the bare feet leading the way. The bare feet that she was following.

The return journey from Aegina was uninteresting. Vaso was absorbed in herself again, in the net that enfolded her body in this strange human landscape.

'Are you happy?' Anna asked her, to make conversation. 'Do you like the place?'

'The earth is dry and small, and surrounded by so much water,' was all she said.

Then she brought out some brown bread from a handkerchief and began to eat it mechanically.

Haritos withdrew to a corner of the prow and looked out to sea. Anna huddled up beside Andreas against the cold and leaned on his shoulder.

'Now...?' she said at some point, softly. 'Now what will happen?'

'You will be my wife,' he replied, 'and I will love you my whole life.'

In his eyes and body she sensed serenity: the thrill of a satisfied animal certain of its prey.

'Keep an eye on the cargo!' Fotis shouted.

He had no reason to fear for the cargo, but he felt the need at that moment, contrary to his habits, to begin talking about his work. He was feeling happy and content.

'Why are you staring at the sea like an idiot!' he shouted at Haritos. 'Come here!'

Haritos got up obediently.

'Well, what do you make of it?' Fotis asked him, meaning the stolen salt that had become jugs from Aegina.

'You know best, captain,' he responded, unwilling to partake in the conversation.

'Of course I do! But what do *you* think?'

'I think it's a job well done.'

'If you're honest and listen to me, we'll be raking it in, you'll see!'

He raised his head and looked around at the sea, surrounded as it was by islands and land. His gaze moved down to Hydra, Sounion, Poros, Aegina, Salamis, the Peloponnese. Then he raised his hand and drew a great circle in the air.

'See how much land you can link with one felucca!' he said in wonder. 'All this can be gold, if we want it. Mark my words!'

With his outstretched hand he drew another circle around the series of lands, and in his eyes condensed the same vision that had once glowed in the eyes of those who are at rest, and have been for thousands of years now, in the land of Anavyssos—his land.

'Do you know about dynamite?' he asked Haritos.

'I do.'

'Are you afraid?'

'No.'

'Very well,' said Fotis, and was silent.

And the wood from the Romanian forests cleaved the water, carrying loneliness, earthenware jugs and dreams.

CHAPTER SEVEN

The roadroller

The travellers returned from Aegina to Anavyssos after nightfall. Fotis expected that people would have gathered on the mole to welcome them, as it was the first spring voyage made by the only local boat, and it should have been an important event for the residents of the shacks.

But no one was waiting.

'How strange,' Fotis murmured as he lowered the sail. His pride was hurt. What was going on?

Vaso spotted it first.

'Look over there!' she said to her husband. 'What's that?'

On the large seaside square belonging to the shacks, a dark mass was visible in the clear night. Voices were coming from around it. And among the voices, thick black smoke was rising high, mingling with sparks.

'Oh!' said Fotis in surprise. 'What's that?'

His mind did not fear the worst. Even if it was fire, their shacks were not in danger as it was an open area.

But what could it be?

It was a demon that had crossed the borders of the hills of Anavyssos and arrived heavy, dark and sooty to add its variety to the story of the shacks.

'What is that?' one white salt pyramid said from the salt pans, when the black mass, belching smoke and fire from its body, appeared on its way down from the hills.

'It's something for them to play with,' said a second, who was wiser and knew the meaning of the world.

It was a great machine made of iron, chains and wheels. It lumbered along making a fearful din, and came to rest in the empty square. A young man with an oilcloth cap, sooty face and bloodshot eyes leapt out of the machine, which had been surrounded by the children and women.

'Who's in charge here?' he asked.

At such times, when the Phocians wanted to appear respectable, they had none other than Doctor Venis.

'We'll go and call him,' they said guardedly.

They ran to find the doctor.

He was digging earth in his rose garden when they informed him of the arrival.

'A strange machine has come, with a sooty man!' they said. 'Come.'

Dimitris ensured he encouraged them first, when he saw they were scared.

'Why are you like that? What are you scared of?'

Yes, why should they be afraid?

He abandoned his pickaxe and went with them to the square.

'Oh, it's a roadroller,' he said, when he approached the machine.

The tone of his voice was so different from the atmosphere of wonder that surrounded the mass of iron and the strange man that he succeeded in rattling its driver.

'What were you expecting? A tank? Of course it's a roadroller! Are you the president?' he asked the doctor abruptly.

'We have no president,' the doctor responded. 'But you can speak to me on behalf of the village. What are you after?'

'We're making a road to connect you with the main town. That's why we came.'

'Well, you are very welcome then! But…'

Unwilling to continue his thought, he paused for a moment. The man did not permit this.

'But what?'

'Are you beginning with the roadroller?' the doctor asked somewhat archly. 'I imagined that they would begin by cutting the road, preparing the stone, and then—'

'Well it's not the first time things are upside down!' he interrupted, affronted. 'Nor will anyone be asking *you* where we should begin.'

'No, I suppose they will not.'

'I'm hungry,' the mechanic said, 'and tired. Is there an inn here?'

'No. People do not usually travel past here. There is no onward road.'

'Then I will eat and sleep at your house,' he said in his brusque manner. 'Go and tell them to prepare for me.'

'Very well, young man,' Dimitris said calmly. 'You will eat and sleep at my house. But do not speak like that.'

The mechanic did not hear, or pretended not to, for he had turned to screw something onto his machine. Then he left it and followed Dimitris' gentle steps.

And when Anna arrived home from the journey with Andreas, they found this new being wandering around in the loneliness of the others.

Irini Venis was livid at this development.

'Is that your daughter?' the mechanic had asked the doctor when he came into the house and saw Irini.

The doctor lowered his eyes, as if it was his fault that she was not his daughter, and said, 'My daughter is on Aegina. She will come in the evening.'

'And who's this?'

'That is my wife,' he said, with effort.

'Oh! It's your wife?' he said, eyeing him leeringly from head to toe.

Irini observed this small scene wordlessly. Then she hurried upstairs and locked herself in her room.

The doctor had to call a neighbour from the next-door shack to look after the man.

'Your daughter is coming back from sea, at night, with the young man! And you bring this dirty, vulgar good-for-nothing to my house! And I am to sit and take it all!' she shouted at her husband. 'What are we coming to?'

'What could possibly go wrong? Calm down, Irini. The girl went to Aegina to have a break, and a stranger has come here to sleep. Why are you being like this?'

'Well, do what you want! Do what you want! But remember, sometime the glass will smash!'

And she used this excuse to tell him again of their sorry state.

'Don't you see what we've become? We're in the worst state of all the villagers! We live off their pity, and they work for us on the assumption that they might get a fever and need our help. Yes, we live off their pity and wait for their fevers!'

'Who's shouting upstairs?' the mechanic asked the Phocian woman, who was preparing eggs.

'It's the lady. The doctor's wife.'

'Why is she doing that?'

'I don't know. They argue every so often.'

'Your lady is just the ticket in a desert like this, eh?' he said.

'You should have seen her as a girl!' the Phocian woman said in wonder. 'But she is still so young and so different from us, with everything she's been through...'

The mechanic asked who else lived in the house.

'Their daughter, Anna. We all say she'll be married to the lad who came from the East,' she added, so as to leave no crease unironed.

'Anyone else?'

'No.'

'Very well.'

And, as if he were the master of the house, he requested that they make his bed on the ground floor.

'Tell me something about your trip, Anna,' Aunt Maria said to the girl that same night.

'It was lovely, Aunt,' was all she said.

She was tired and wanted to sleep, to be alone with herself.

'Now…?' she had asked Andreas. 'I will love you my whole life,' he had replied. Now she closed her eyes and said again to herself, 'I will love you my whole life.'

· ·

He walked a lot and became tired. It was evening when he reached the cave on Mount Latmus. He fell into a deep sleep. Then the great god came and said, 'What do you want your life to be? Tell me.' Endymion asked never to die but to remain there, submerged in an endless sleep. And so it was: he remained there, submerged in an endless sleep. Every evening the moon came and fell next to him and caressed him, and the leaves of the forest whispered to him.

Then, with the stones and the road, an unusual commotion overtook the small plain of Anavyssos. All
those not working on the land began to smash stones
to make gravel on behalf of the company constructing
the road. Other destitute people from the places
behind the hills found out about this blessing and
came to earn their daily bread. It was tough work, even
if it did not appear so. As the hammer endlessly strikes
the same point on the shattering stone, it loses its aim;
it strikes right, then left, then on the fingers. The light
torments the small gap between stone and eye, alters it,
fills it with sparks, stars and blood. And when evening
starts to fall, it fills it with exhaustion and pain.

Vaso got ready in the morning, prayed, gave food to
the children and said to her husband, 'With your per-
mission, I'm going there as well. We are all one family.'

Fotis had not thought of this. But when he saw she
was prepared, he did not disapprove.

'Very well. You may go.'

And when he saw her go, he thought how well he
had chosen. *Those* are real women! Strong and hard-
working!

He tried to think why the others, their own women
from the coast, were another species: less disciplined,
more fickle. But it was uninteresting to him, and Fotis
was not used to wasting his time on such meaningless
things. He thought of his next journey on the *Eleni* to
Poros. I must find dynamite, he thought. The goal was
clear. With dynamite you can fill the boat with fish

at night, and at dawn you're at Sounion, where the fishmonger is waiting.

'Torment your body,' Dimitris Venis had told him. And it was simple folk-wisdom speaking through his mouth.

'Tomorrow I'm going to go to the road as well, Anna,' Andreas announced.

She understood immediately.

'I'll come too, to keep you company.'

No, he did not want her to. It was not heavy work. He would work there until something better turned up that he could do. Then he would see how they could be married.

'I have done this work back at home,' he added, so she would not think him unversed in stone, and pity him.

CHAPTER EIGHT

Irini Venis, the mechanic and the fantasies

Irini Venis returned late at night from the rocks. She believed in nothing and expected nothing. Yet, without realising it, her very disbelief and loneliness engendered an indefinable feeling, creating the balance that life demands. 'Something might happen in spring,' the mystical voice said. What would happen? Who knew? But the desolation of winter would leave, the rain would stop. She would no longer be forced to sit day and night surrounded by four low walls, body and soul trapped in bitter isolation. Something else might happen: they might leave, be taken elsewhere, or there might be war and a return to their land, or fevers might come from the marshes.

But spring came and nothing changed, nothing apart from a halt to the rain. All the residents of the shacks silently accepted their fate. Will this, then, be the end? Everything contends that it will. The vines they planted have sprouted green leaves. Around their shacks, the refugees have made pens for their animals, which have multiplied: one has become two, then three, then small flocks. They grazed them on the new grass and ploughed the fallow land. Near Fotis' windmill, that winged toy, there was now another windmill, and others, in preparation for drought. Women became pregnant again, and in a few months children would be born, seeds of this land. Peace was now final and the refugees would never return to their homes.

The fevers did not come. 'We live in wait of them,' Irini had said to the doctor, 'for the people work for us on the assumption that they might get a fever and need our help.' They did not come, as Dimitris Venis embarked on his crusade, driving the people to cover the marsh, cut channels and drain the water into the sea.

Most significantly, however, everyone was now used to the place. Everything was done with certainty and for the long term. 'Do you feel the loneliness surrounding you?' the young man with gold on his shoulders and a beautiful face had asked little Irini on that long night. A small English warship had entered their harbour, as every year, and the consul was invited that night to a reception given by the ship's captain. It was summer, Irini put on a white dress and went with her father to the ship. 'No. Why would I feel lonely?' she replied. 'I travel wherever I want. Our country is beautiful. I have a horse…' 'I beg your pardon,' said the blond young man, 'I did not mean to slight your country.' They spoke on the bridge, with the night over them. 'Will you come next year?' the young girl with the white dress asked.

'Perhaps.' 'And will you take me with you on the seas?' she asked with a smile. 'Who knows?' he answered.

. . . .

Irini Venis arrived at their house out of breath, for the night had thickened outside and she was suddenly afraid. She saw the light on the ground floor. The mechanic must have returned, she thought. And she felt the same bitter, hostile sentiment overtaking her, as it had the first time he had remarked to her, 'You, my lady, are a divine thing.' None of the villagers had ever dared to look at her without respect, or to see her as a woman. She fled upstairs and asked the doctor, without saying why, to expel the barbarian from their house immediately.

'No, it's not right,' he had replied. 'Let's wait for the weather to improve. Then he can sleep outside.'

'Watch out or you'll regret it.'

'I don't think so,' he replied.

And since then the mechanic had not stopped his pursuit.

One night he said, 'When they're asleep upstairs, come down. It'll be nice.'

Now she avoided his eye. She shuddered at his coarseness. Gradually she stopped responding to him. But something was stirring inside her—a great upheaval —her strength gathering day by day, like a procession of storks.

'When will he leave?' she had asked the doctor again, a few days previously.

'Sometime…' he answered in his saintly manner.

Irini continued to the small entrance to the house and cast a quick glance in his direction. The mechanic had washed and was drying himself. She tried to hurry past, but he stopped her.

'Have you come from far?'

'Leave me alone,' she said brusquely.

'I just want to know how the rocks and the holly bushes are getting on,' he said. 'Anyway, what are you doing wasting your time over at the rocks?'

Her lips trembled with anger. Was this woman really the girl in white under the lights of the ship? 'Will you take me with you on the seas when you come back?' 'Perhaps.' And on that night the stars had snuffed themselves out in the roof of the world, saying, 'Down there is little Irini, talking about the seas…' 'What did he say to her?' one star asked. 'He said "perhaps".' 'Well, let's go then. They are preparing for their journey with dreams. They do not need us now.' So spoke the two stars, and left, and the others followed them and tumbled into the icy depths.

'Let me past!' Irini shouted to the mechanic, who had blocked her way. 'Brute!'

'Will you come tonight?' he insisted, ignoring her. 'It's your last chance. And I know you're *starving*. I'm leaving tomorrow!'

He was leaving tomorrow? Yes, it was one of the paradoxes of the place: before the work on the road had really begun, they found there was greater need for the roadroller in Chalkis, on another road the same company was making.

'You'll regret it,' he said. 'I'm leaving tomorrow! I'm leaving! Will you come?'

She rushed at him, shoved him out of the way and ran up the few stairs that led to the upper floor.

The family was gathered around the light of the poor lamp, and the blessedness brought by Dimitris Venis' existence glowed on all their faces.

What were they talking about?

Anna, Aunt Maria and Andreas were there.

'Have you come from far?' Dimitris Venis asked her. 'It's late.'

She sat down to draw breath and did not reply.

'Have you come from far?' Dimitris asked her again.

'From there!' she answered tersely, pointing towards the rocks.

'We saw you going past. I was in the rose garden with Anna. Did you see us?'

No, she had not seen them.

'Well, I can announce to you…' the doctor began slowly, smiling in his gentle way.

She turned and looked at him with her piercing gaze. 'What?'

He took a deep breath and stressed the words one by one: 'The canes have taken. The roses will grow.'

All eyes turned to Irini.

'As I thought,' Dimitris said. 'In the dry earth, with all this salt…'

'As I thought,' he repeated, and his voice tried to hide the deep notes wanting to burst out of the satisfied beast. 'Well?'

He now fixed his eyes on his wife, who was sitting in her corner like a hunted animal, surrounded on all sides.

'Well?'

'Oh. They've taken root…' she muttered.

'Yes, they have!' Dimitris said again in a hostile, pitiless manner.

They sat there, rallied around him, her daughter and sister, a series of eyes that grew wider and filled the room, as if looking for her to take some responsibility.

'And everything will end up as I planned,' continued the voice mercilessly. 'Ask Andreas. You'll see.'

No reply.

'You've found peace, child. Is that not so?' the doctor asked.

'Yes,' he answered softly, as if hypnotised.

'And Angelos will come back one of these days,' said Aunt Maria, elated, moved by the atmosphere of faith and fantasy that filled the room.

Three pairs of eyes—Andreas', Anna's and the doctor's—met each other.

'Yes, he will return one of these days,' Dimitris repeated firmly. 'And we will all be happy here, until the end. Is that not so, Anna?'

'Just so, Father.'

'Andreas?'

'Just so.'
'Maria?'
'Just so, Dimitris.'

Night came deep and the desolation thick in the earth of Anavyssos. The hills that enclosed the land grew terrifyingly tall and hid the stars from the south and north and from where the sun rises. The land became a prison. The hands of men furiously dug the earth, which had been dormant for centuries. The earth gradually took shape, became a tomb: the most certain shape. 'And we will all be happy *here, until the end,*' Dimitris Venis had said. Until the end. And his voice had a hostile tone, like that of all prophets.

For the first time in their life together, Irini Venis was discovering this tone. And she discovered it in the prophecy of their end. 'Come here, at last,' the voice said to her. 'In all the years that have passed, you have tyrannised my days. You have thought of no one but yourself. My body was bound to yours, but it remained foreign and alone. And my mind and heart, just the same—foreign and alone—slipped past your heart and mind. Up there, when the time comes, they will ask you, "Who did you meet on earth?" And you will respond, "No one. Only myself." Then they will ask you, "Did you at least believe in dreams and fantasies, in the humble works of humble people?" And you will reply, "No." "And did you pay for that down there?" And you must reply that yes, you paid for it, for human

fate lies here on earth. Come then to this land, enclosed by hills. Come and bloody your hands: a tomb
is being prepared, and you will dig it alone.'

In the middle of the night Irini Venis got up. Everyone
in the house had fallen asleep. Her eyes were wide,
were leaping out of their sockets. A powerful spasm
shook her body.

'Oh, that… no… no…'

Dimitris was deep in blessed sleep next to her. She
heard his soft breathing. He must be smiling in his
sleep. Suddenly she felt a deep, unbearable hatred
rising in her for that sleeping body, so calm and com-
posed. She got up slowly, put on some clothes, opened
the door and went down the stairs.

The mechanic was asleep. In the darkness she could
make out his body. She hesitated a moment, then went
resolutely towards him and prodded him.

'Get up!'

'Oh, it's you. Come on then!' he said, rubbing his
sleepy eyes and stretching out his hand to pull her in.

'Get up!' she commanded.

She waited for him to put on his clothes, opened
the door, and they went into the night.

'What is it?' asked the mechanic, perplexed.

But she simply ran. She ran and ran. The night was
cold, yet her body was drenched in sweat. She leapt
hypnotically over the ditches and the mounds of earth,
and kept running. At some point she tripped and

fell. She got up silently and continued her panicked course.

They had reached the rose garden. Irini hesitated there for a moment, among the roots resting in the earth, which was peacefully preparing the powers of life inside it. Then she leaned down, wrapped her hands around the first cane she saw, and pulled it hard. She hurried on and yanked another one. Then, driven by her fury, she began to uproot one after the other in the darkness.

'Pull!' she shouted desperately at the mechanic, behind her. 'Pull!'

Blood ran from her hands but she felt nothing.

'Pull!' she groaned. 'Pull!'

Surprised at first, then rather amused at this curiosity, he put his back into it.

'Here we go!' he said, and began pulling up the roses.

Their task took a long time. Finally, worn out and bloody, Irini fell face down on the earth. Her breath was short and hard. And the mechanic shouted over the fallen body, 'She'll have a good old time with the old man when he comes here in the morning!'

Then he grabbed her body and turned it, face to face with his, towards the sky. He made to remove her clothes, but she stopped him with her last remaining strength.

'Not now. Have pity,' she begged. 'Tomorrow, do what you like with me.'

Her voice had a deep anguish, which reached to the heart of the roused animal and softened it.

'Tomorrow I'm leaving,' he said, unwilling to abandon his prey altogether. 'Stop, won't you!'

'I'll come with you,' she said softly.

'What do you mean? Where will you go?'

She'll go anywhere. He can do whatever he wants with her and leave her wherever he wants. She will ask nothing of him. She cannot stay here, after the night's deed.

'Oh, it's like that, is it? Look, I'm always on the move, laying roads. What'll I do with you?'

'I'll come!' she said again, and her voice had found its severe tone. 'On the other side of the mountains you can be in charge and do whatever you want with me. You can leave me...'

The mechanic saw where this was going. It was not half bad. What if he took her with him to the roads of Chalkis? She wasn't exactly a helpless little girl. He would have no trouble. If he tired of her, he would issue her marching orders.

'Let's go now!' said Irini.

'But it's the middle of the night!'

'That is why we must go now.'

She got up.

'I will go to the machine,' she said, 'and wait for you there.'

'Won't you take anything with you?'

No, she cannot return home now.

The damp soil pulled out with the roots of the roses smelled strong. A worm, which had followed the root on its unexpected upward journey and was surprised by the sight of the world, now looked for refuge in the earth again.

. . . .

Aunt Maria was awoken by the great din that suddenly filled the stillness of the night.

'What is it?' she wondered, and sat up on her mattress.

'What is it?' Anna asked, waking with a start.

Then she remembered. 'Oh! The roadroller is leaving,' she said. 'It's nothing.'

Then she turned over and fell asleep, and the muffled sound was lost in the night.

CHAPTER NINE

Anna

The sun had just appeared above the hills of Anavyssos. Anna woke up and rubbed her eyes.

'Oh! It was a dream…'

A dream it may have been, but it was so beautiful!
The earth was glowing white and red and blue. It was
summer. The land seemed open on all sides without
limit, although on one side high white walls fenced the
horizon. They were neither mountains, nor cliffs. They
were something else, like a thick foam that had dried
and become a solid mass. Even though she could go
towards the open land, Anna made for the white walls
instead. For young Anna Venis felt the powers of life
sparkling inside her. When she came close to these
white blocks, she tried but could not understand
which beings of the world they resembled. Nonetheless, they seemed good, and she asked them, 'What is
behind there?'

They replied, 'Are you Anna Venis?'

'Yes, I am.'

'Then come and look.'

The white walls gave way and Anna saw the unknown place behind them.

The earth beyond was neither blue, nor red nor white. It was gold. Strange golden birds were singing, sailing through the place, which was gleaming with golden reflections. An unknown music emerged from deep within.

'Where is the music coming from?' Anna asked the white blocks.

'Oh, from very far away!'

'Are there people singing over there?'

'There are, but not many.'

'Why not many?'

The white walls replied that only once in a thousand years did they give way for one—only one—person to go into the land of the golden birds.

'Is it nearly a thousand years since the last person?' Anna asked.

'Today marks a thousand years.'

'If it is so, my good white friends, let me go through!'

'But we were waiting for you!'

She crouched down and said in hushed tones, 'Can I take Andreas with me? He's the young man who loves me.'

But the white walls answered sadly, 'No, Anna. That won't do. You will go alone.'

Then she told them to close the passage to the land of the golden birds and wait another thousand years for the one destined to go, for she would not go alone.

The good, white blocks closed the passage and said in surprise, 'This has never happened before. Until now, no one has seen the golden land and turned away. Do you love him that much, Anna?'

'I do.'

She ran to her parents' room, to find her father.

'Have you seen your mother?' he asked her.

'No, Father. She must have gone for a morning walk. It's a beautiful day!'

'Indeed it is.'

'Did the sound of the machine leaving wake you up?'

No, it did not. He slept deeply.

'At last it's gone,' added Dimitris with relief. 'Your mother will be pleased.'

She nodded.

'I'm going over there, Father,' Anna said, pointing to where they were making the road. 'Perhaps even a little further.'

On such a beautiful day, it would be lovely in the woods on the hills, beyond the salt pyramids.

'I'll bring you some greens, Father. There are a lot over there.'

She felt a strange joy flooding her, a powerful wave of optimism and gentleness. She leaned down and kissed her father on the forehead.

'Are you happy, Anna?'

'I am, Father.'

She kissed Aunt Maria too.

She did not usually kiss them when she went out. The old woman was surprised.

'Where are you going?' she asked, smiling. 'Are you off on a journey?'

'Let's call it a journey, Aunt!' she replied joyfully. 'A journey for greens, in a golden land!'

The road workers had got to know her. She went every day, sat on the piles of broken stones made by Andreas and encouraged him.

'You'll see, you'll see what will come of these stones!' she said, clasping a few in her hands.

'What will, Anna?'

'A man!' she replied, looking at him seriously. 'So Father says. And I have blind faith in him.'

Andreas would abandon his work for a few moments while they chatted. The road supervisor had initially scolded him, but such was the spring joy the girl brought with her to their harsh landscape that he became used to her and smiled when she came.

'He's there,' he would say when he saw her, pointing to where Andreas was working.

She thanked him with a wave and ran to her friend, passing through the two lines of men striking the rock at the edges of the road. And all the anguished faces turned towards this vision and smiled.

'Good morning, sweetheart!'

'Good morning, sweetheart!'

Vaso was the only woman working with them in their strenuous labour. After seeing Andreas, Anna always sat awhile with her and talked to her. And when Anna left, the hammers struck the stone with a quicker rhythm and the supervisor was happy.

'You're early!' Andreas said when she sat beside him on the stones.

'I'm going to gather greens for Father,' she said breezily. 'I want to thank him.'

'But what has happened?' he asked, noticing the glow in her face.

What has happened? Last night Anna rejected the land of the golden birds. Every thousand years one, only one, person goes in, and yet she refused. And the good white walls that guarded the passage told her that had never happened before.

She told Andreas about her sacrifice.

'I did it for you,' she said sweetly, smiling.

He laughed gaily and teased her: 'But it was a dream! You made a sacrifice for me in a dream.'

Then the smile left her face and she suddenly became serious.

'It makes no difference,' she said. 'I believe in dreams as if they were life itself.'

Andreas concentrated his thoughts onto one point and his good humour vanished at once.

'Did you say it was all gold there, in your dream?'

'Yes. Why do you ask?'

But Andreas was now travelling back to the days in the East, to the final night with Angelos and the golden mud.

He felt something inexplicable clench his heart.

'Don't go to the mountains,' he begged her.

Anna could not understand.

'What do you mean?' she cried, finding her humour again. 'Why should I not go on such a day? I promised my father I would bring him greens. I'm going!'

He did not know how to explain himself.

She got up and bid him farewell.

'Goodbye, Andreas!'

'Goodbye, Anna!'

Then she passed Vaso and smiled at her, stroking her back.

'Goodbye, Vaso!'

She bid goodbye to all the people on the road.

'Goodbye! Goodbye!'

And God's blossoming spring remained there among them, long after she had left, until the joyful, moving spot disappeared behind the white salt pyramids.

Haritos was walking slowly. He had been walking for four hours. He was returning from the other end of this stretch of coast, from Varkiza and Vouliagmeni. He had gone the day before to look for dynamite, as he and Fotis had planned. The fishing boat was going to make a fortune.

Haritos found no dynamite in Varkiza or Vouliagmeni. They seemed not to trust him enough to give it to him. He slept there that night for a few hours, waking when the morning star appeared, and took the road back to Anavyssos. Through the rest of the cold night his mind worked over great ideas: could he perhaps, at some point, be the captain of a boat of his own, with a deckhand? He imagined, on some trip, the weather casting him onto a wasteland on one of the many islands of the Aegean. Captain Haritos alights with the deckhand, and they clamber onto the rocks to find a sheltered place to light a fire for their soup. And there, among the jagged rocks, they find a strange passage, like a footpath. Haritos takes the path, and the deckhand follows. Someone has been here before, he thinks. Of course someone had been there before! At the end of the path, a huge wall, a fearful rock, suddenly blocks their way. Haritos examines it, wondering at its grandeur. Then, at the height of his head, he sees that the rock has a rectangular fissure in it, as if a slab has been put there to enclose a cavity. Strange! he thinks. He rolls down a rock to stand on, reaches the level of the crack, and sends the deckhand to the boat for a small crowbar. It's tricky, but when he finally manages to remove the stone covering the cavity, a vaulted path appears in the heart of the rock. Haritos leaves the deckhand to wait and goes in. It's pitch black in there.

But he does not need to go very far: his feet trip over an obstacle. He bends down and fumbles around, and his heart starts racing. There, at his feet, is a small wooden chest. He shatters it with the crowbar. He puts his hands into the open chest, and his fingers make the sleeping gold jangle. He plunges them in as far as they can go, but he cannot find the bottom, so great is the buried pirate treasure. What now? If only the deckhand wasn't here, he thinks, then I would be the only one to know the secret of the rock. At that moment, in the darkness of the damp cave and amid the sound of the gold, a thought flashes through his mind: kill him? Merely at the thought a cold sweat comes over him. No! A thousand times no! How did it cross his mind to kill a person, let alone a child? He, Haritos, could never do that.

. . . .

The sun rose over the coast of Attica, driving away the dew, the treasure and the rocks, and bringing humbler things into Haritos' mind: how nice it would be if his captain, Fotis, let him run the boat once a month, and take whatever fish he caught that day! Who can know the will of God? One of those days, just one, Haritos might come across a passing shoal of fish. What wealth, then, what happiness would arrive! Yes, that could happen. Anything can happen down here in this world. Anything.

. . . .

Haritos had now reached the pine woods on the three hills that separate the plain of Anavyssos from the region of Vari. No one goes through it. All is desolate, and deathly silence reigns. On the virginal earth, where the dry leaves have made a thick layer, the footsteps of a barefoot man vanish.

Haritos felt happy. He was whistling. He skirted a small rise and found himself suddenly in a clearing surrounded by pines. Only in the west did serene light open towards the Saronic Gulf and Fleves. On that side, a few metres beyond, the body of a girl was crouched on the ground, head down and two young, bare legs showing.

'Hullo!' said Haritos, stopping in front of this vision of joy.

His voice filled the serenity. The crouched body stood up and its bare legs trod more firmly on the ground. Anna turned, frightened, 'Oh, it's you.'

Then, recognising his insignificant existence, she immediately recovered herself.

'I was afraid…' she muttered.

Then, louder, she asked, 'Where are you going?'

'I'm returning from Vari to Anavyssos. You?'

'I am gathering greens.'

'Oh, greens…'

What if he gathered some too?

'Well, goodbye!' Anna said, and bent down again, indifferently.

No reply. One minute passed, then another.

The girl's body rose again. She turned around, curious as to why he had not said goodbye.

'You're still here?'

'Yes. I'll gather some greens too.'

'Fine.'

Anna leaned down again. She was on an uphill slope, and as she leaned, more of her bare legs above the knee was revealed. Her firm flesh gleamed with vigour. How much must the wave swell? Haritos stooped to pull up one of the wild greens, struggling to avoid his attraction, but the naked light is there, just above him—her knees. His eyes are fixed, cunning and fearful. He lowers them. They return of their own accord. How much must the wave swell? It rises slowly, hot, burning, to his shaggy face, paints it, pollutes the blood, pollutes the mind. Serenity is all around, a deathly loneliness, the whole place a naked body.

His eyes are now burning. He moves slowly towards her.

She hears his steps, their light rustle on the dry pine needles.

She stands up, turns to look at him.

'What is it?'

Her eyes meet his, search in them, try to guess.

'What is it?' Anna asks again, unable to imagine.

But the hostile body gives no reply. His pores, his blood, bones and flesh have become memory. They see nothing but a distant image from the stream on Aegina, under the tree: the naked girl moaning, and above her, her friend moaning too.

'What is it?' Anna asks a third time and, suddenly, looking into the eye of the beast standing before her, she understands and screams.

He leaps onto her.

'Come here!'

She makes a desperate attempt to escape. She starts running, and her cries are heart-rending: 'Help! Help!'

But Haritos, more ferocious now, catches up with her, grabs her again and throws her onto the ground. The feel of the young body stirs his blood yet more.

'Stay still!' he roars. 'Stay still like you did for him!'

Her cries become louder and louder. She struggles to escape, he struggles to hold her. Mustering all her strength, Anna manages to half get up, grab a stone in her hands and strike him across the face. Then he, now in a frenzy, seizes her hand, twists it and, with the same stone, begins to strike her across the head manically. He strikes and strikes. Blood gushes out and spatters his face, and he keeps striking until her cries die down and become a rattling, plaintive breath.

Then, free now, having conquered her resistance, Haritos strips the young girl and has his way with her, and his groans cover her breath and her whimpers, which gradually disappear in the serenity of the hillside.

Haritos got up. He looked at Anna. No movement. Just her body at his feet, naked from the waist down and gleaming in the sun. Her blood was gleaming too.

The animal sighed deeply with satisfaction.

'Ah...'

He turned to look again at the bloodied face. But then came something new and unknown, preventing him from looking: fear.

He backed away slowly, terrified, quickening his step, then began to run like a hunted animal. He saw nothing before him. At some point he tripped on a bush, slipped and fell. He got up and touched his face: his hands were covered in blood. A green leaf, the only one he had gathered, had stuck to his hand in the commotion and was steeped in blood, like a strange red snake. He detached it from his hand and threw it away in disgust. And when he realised, only then, that his face was covered in the spattered blood of the girl, he began to run again, without turning to look behind him.

How long did he run for?

He became tired. Before him now was the well. Anna had once stopped with Zabeta at the same well and had begged God to bring her someone. Haritos was parched. He looked around for a bucket. There was none. The shepherds were not in those parts at that time of year. They had taken their bucket.

He leaned into the well. In the still water of the deeps he thought he saw his head—shaken, fearful, with its tough, straight hair.

Water, he thought. Water... water...

He looked closer at the well. It was made artlessly, with the stones protruding here and there, giving him footholds.

He began to descend, afraid at first, then with more confidence. The coolness of the water, emerging from the deeps, felt good. A little further…

At last he was there. The image in the water was trembling. He broke it with his hands and washed his face. He drank. Then he went up again to the ground.

Now he felt better, but he realised how tired he was. He sat under a tree. A light wind blew. There was nothing: no recollection, no trace. Everything was mixed up, confused inside him; the sun fell on him and a deep tiredness overcame him.

He turned over and fell asleep.

Dimitris Venis found out late about the destruction in the rose garden. A boy, passing through the field, saw it and ran to tell him.

'The roses are uprooted! The roses are uprooted! They're all lying on the ground!'

'What's happened?' he said.

He arrived in a fury at the field of fantasies. The canes with their green buds were lying there broken. The damp, dark earth from their roots had started to dry in the open air. It was the end.

Dimitris' hands trembled, his voice in vain tried to put syllables together and give meaning to this anguish.

'Who did this? What beast could do this?'

He turned each of the dead canes upwards—those little fantasies—and fondled them as if speaking to them, as if each had its own individual story known only to him. Now that they had died he wanted, one final time, to tell that story, as happens with the dead.

'How I suffered for you… How I hoped in you…' he said to the shoots.

The first person he thought of was Anna.

'Where are you now, my darling? How will you be able to look upon this?'

Anna! Anna! When will you come back, little Anna, if only to see this? When will you come back?

Afternoon came and no one appeared. Neither Irini nor Anna. Late afternoon. The sun had started to lean on the mountains of Aegina, when the shock of disaster passed through the shacks of Anavyssos like lightning.

'Irini Venis has disappeared! Anna has disappeared! The rose canes have been uprooted.'

The terror passed over the shacks, reached the road workers and the young man struggling to find serenity again. It came like a cloud and crushed them. The hammers stopped striking and the stones waited for the blow. In the stones there still remained the spirit of the morning joy that had come and gone, that little vision, a coloured skirt and glowing face. Was it not that morning she had gone past and said goodbye?

Then at once the cloud lifted, the hammers struck the ground and the road workers leapt up. The supervisor tried to check them in vain.

'What are we waiting for? What are we waiting for? We know the girl went that way! Let's find her!'

And the people of the shacks, the road workers, along with Andreas and Dimitris Venis, streamed towards the place beyond the salt pyramids. Haritos followed.

Only Fotis Glaros did not go with them. He had travelled inland the day before in search of a plough. Not finding one at a good price, he was returning when, walking alone on the road, he heard from afar the sound of the roadroller coming along the same road on its way to other parts.

'Oh, bra-vo! He really worked hard for us!' he said smiling, mocking the topsy-turvy things that happen in this place.

They continued in the sun—the vehicle from one direction, he from the other. But then he gave a start. There seemed to be two figures at the wheel. One, of course, was the driver. But the other? His curiosity grew.

'Doesn't the other one look like a woman?'

At length they met. Fotis gave way on the side of the road. He paused. Then, with eyes full of surprise, bewilderment and fear, he saw Irini Venis riding on the heavy iron of the vehicle, her head resting on the driver's shoulder, asleep and ghostly white. The vehicle was making a demonic din as it ascended the difficult incline that led out of the ring of hills.

When Fotis returned to the shacks of Anavyssos in the afternoon, the news had spread: 'Irini Venis has disappeared! Anna has disappeared! The roses have been uprooted!'

In Fotis' mind, the three facts at once merged into one, as fate binds people in their joys and woes. Lacking information, he sought an explanation. Nothing. The only thing that came before his eyes, the only cause, the beginning of it all—it must be—was the departing woman, Irini Venis. And the only thing that remained unbearably, severely wounded was the good man, Dimitris Venis.

Ah, it's like that is it? Such a person will be ruined, hour by hour, at her whim? he thought.

Saying nothing to anyone, not even Vaso, he went to ask his neighbour for a horse. The neighbour was not there, so he took the horse without asking, mounted and galloped off on the road taken by the vehicle, hunting the treacherous woman.

And the salt pyramids, seeing all the fuss, wondered, 'What is it?'

'Nothing. They're just playing.'

They found Anna in her blood, her nakedness, after the sun had set. Dimitris saw her first. Such was the will of the road he followed. He collapsed onto her, onto her blood, which had now congealed, and covered his hands and face with it.

'Who could do this to you, my darling? Who, my angel? To think, I was worried about you seeing the uprooted roses...'

All around him, mute in their anguish, the wretches from the shacks looked at the body tangled up in death and fate. Unable to reach an explanation for this will of heaven, they had forgotten themselves such that no one had asked who could have done it.

Among the crowd yet alone, leaning over the tangle of the good man and his daughter, Anna's friend Andreas stood in silence, his face distorted with a grief that had taken on the colour of death. He looked speechlessly at the unbearable sight. No movement, no tears, nothing. Those are only for the calamities that can be reckoned in human terms.

'Let's go, Father…' he stammered at last.

He helped up the wreck that was Dimitris Venis. Then he bent down to lift the girl's dead body. Three others went to help. Andreas bent down. He made to put his hand under her head, under her back. Slowly. He touched her. Slowly. Then, like an animal held and suddenly released, he fell on her, embracing the beloved head, and started to kiss it, quivering uncontrollably.

Four people lifted Anna.

Two took her legs, while Andreas and another had her shoulders. Two others hauled her father along. And behind followed the wild and silent crowd of Phocians.

The procession advanced. Night fell. What sweet colours of evening! Andreas walked slowly, his arms wrapped around Anna's shoulder. Her head hung limp. He put his hand underneath to support it, looking straight in front, not at her head. He monitored its position by touch. He walked. Slower. Past the salt pyramids. And yet, in her sleep yesterday, Anna did not want to pass the white walls. So she had told him. For his love. Why, then, did she pass them today? Why?

His knees buckled. The colours of evening, the salt, the trees, her hair—everything merged.

'He's falling!' cried one of the crowd, seeing him buckle. '*You* hold her!' he shouted to Haritos, who was walking, huddled and silent, next to Andreas.

And he, Haritos, timidly approached when Andreas had slumped down, and just managed to grab the girl's shoulder with his trembling hands.

Aunt Maria received Anna when they brought her in, instead of her mother. She, Vaso and Aunt Sophia washed the sweet face, the dark hair, and put her in another, lighter dress.

'Where is her mother?' they said in their lamentation. 'Where is her mother?'

From instinct, from their subconscious intuition of things, no one suspected death. No one was afraid for Irini Venis. Only her husband sought her.

'Where are you, Irini, at a time like this? What will you find when you return, you poor thing?'

It was not long before she came. Fotis' horse galloped in and stopped outside the lighted shack of

Dimitris Venis. Fotis lifted her off and set her down. The crowd parted for her. They looked at her with hostility and hatred, knowing nothing of her flight, but seeking the reason for Anna's fate. She walked up the stairs trembling, towards the laid-out young body, still knowing nothing. Until, finally, she saw.

Then the whole world—the waters, the iron of the machine, the gold-buttoned *kavass* of her childhood years, the night with the uprooted roses, everything— became a circle that spun and whistled demonically.

The local governor came and conducted interrogation on interrogation. All suspicions fell on the shepherds of the surrounding mountains. They took in many of them, but found no clear evidence.

Who, then, was guilty?

Fotis sat up awake at night, turning it over in his mind, bringing together his suspicions, then banishing them as unacceptable. Oh, neither God nor man could stand such a thing in the shacks of the Phocians! Who- ever did it must be found!

Fotis turned over his suspicions again.

Could it be?

'But no, no, it could not!' he said to himself. 'A quiet boy like that…'

And yet, only he had passed that place on the day it happened. Haritos. Fotis knew, and only he knew, for the task of the dynamite, on which Haritos had been sent, was secret and must remain so.

'Come here!' he said one day when they were tar-ring the boat. 'Sit down!'

Haritos sat next to him on the sand, his eyes down-cast. Fotis asked, 'What time did you return from Varkiza that day?'

'In the morning.'

'Did you take a path?'

'No, there is none.'

'So you passed the place?'

Fotis' eyes sought the drooping face.

'Which place?' Haritos said timidly.

'The place the girl was killed.'

Haritos replied quickly, fearfully, 'No, I did not.'

Then he got up, to avoid the subject, and went to the boat.

Fotis lay awake that night. The next day, in the af-ternoon, he said to Haritos, 'Come with me.'

The two proceeded silently, passed the salt pyra-mids and made for the woods.

'Where are we going?' Haritos asked, more and more uneasy.

'To work!'

Haritos, however, saw where they were going. He guessed the danger. But he said nothing. He had to remain silent.

Finally they reached the serene place where they had found Anna in her blood.

'Stay here a moment,' Fotis said. 'I'm going to re-lieve myself. I'll be back shortly.'

Evening fell. Darkness came. The branches waved among the trees, their movements drawing strange shapes. The shadows of the forest thickened, the sounds became clearer, each one echoing. And the desolation… Desolation was all around!

Alone, in the shadows and with the voice of the night forest, Haritos stood next to *the place*. He did not dare to look there while it was still light. But it gradually darkened and the voice inside him became more commanding: 'Look! Look *there*!'

No, no! Don't look! But the voice is stronger than the will of men.

'Look! Look there! *There*!'

Defeated at last, he turned his head slowly, timidly, towards the place where the terrible deed had been done.

Then, suddenly, from the surrounding bushes in which he had hidden, Fotis rushed out. The snapping of the branches made a terrifying racket. He seized Haritos by his chest and shook him like a feather, crying, 'Say it, then! Do you not fear God? It was you! You!'

Paralysed by fear, by surprise, by the cries, by the night, by the place, surrounded by nightmares, he began to tremble and fell at Fotis' feet.

'I didn't mean to, captain, I didn't mean to,' he wailed, crying like a baby.

'You dog! How could you!' roared Fotis.

They were almost back at the shacks.

'Whatever clothes you have, I will bring to you in prison,' Fotis said. It was the first thing he had said on the way back.

'Let me go, captain,' he begged. 'I will leave this place and no one will find out. Pity me!'

But Fotis was simple and just and God-fearing.

'Everything is paid here on earth,' was all he said. 'You will pay!'

CHAPTER TEN

Final moment

Summer came. Autumn came too.

How time passed!

Andreas was standing beside old Dimitris, who was sitting on the earth in the field of fantasies. How many years have passed over that good man in so few months? He sat there with a small pickaxe trembling in his hands.

'I came to bid you goodbye once again, Father. I'm leaving shortly.'

Oh, so he was going? Yes, of course he was. He had said goodbye yesterday, too. He would move to a foreign country to seek his fortune. It was decided.

'Farewell, child…' stuttered old Dimitris with emotion. 'Godspeed.'

The young man leaned down to kiss Dimitris' hands. He paused.

'Why…?'

He began to ask, but stopped short.

'Why,' he said at last, 'don't you leave this now?'

'This?'

'Yes, the earth,' he said, indicating the earth that Dimitris had begun to dig again for his roses, to pass the hours of his tragedy.

'Oh, this...' said the old man. 'This... of course...'

A moment passed.

'There is nothing else, child,' he said, more softly.

Then, 'And now there is no one who believes,' he murmured, turning his head.

At the same moment, on the coast path leading to the rocks, two women wrapped in black clothes were walking slowly. It was the same route that Aunt Maria and Anna used to take, speaking about the passing ships.

'I'm tired,' Irini Venis said.

'Let's sit here,' said the other woman, her older sister.

The wave came and broke over their feet, rippling and foaming.

Much time passed. Each of the black-clad women was deep in thought.

'Now...' the older sister said at some point. 'Now we are even. You will have nothing, Irini, to reproach me for.'

'What do you mean?' said Irini.

'Our pasts,' her older sister replied. 'They have become so alike.'

EPILOGUE

Anavyssos is a place in a remote bay in the Saronic Gulf. Once it was the place where the ancient inhabitants of the region laid their dead to rest. Many centuries went by, many layers of earth covered the tombstones and the dead bodies, and nothing remained in the memory of the people about the desolate country. Now, in the same place, Phocian refugees from the East have set up their shacks. They dug the earth and planted vines, and in the summers the plain is green, where once grew only rushes and shrubs.

Avgi is Fotis' youngest child. She was left to him by his first wife, Eleni, when she died. She is one of the youngest inhabitants of the shacks. When Avgi came to Anavyssos she knew nothing about life. Nor does she remember anything from the world outside the borders of the hills that enclose the plain of Anavyssos. That is why she often sits and wonders what could be behind them.

But as she does not know anything of the world and its great cities, she imagines that behind the mountains there is a great pit, deep and desolate, and if you stray from the peaks and fall, nothing can save you; you will die and the black birds will come to eat your body.

Avgi, therefore, has a mystical fear of what is behind the hills of Anavyssos.

Every time she sees her father, Fotis, heading that way to dig the earth they have been given, the mystical fear overcomes her and she wants to say, 'Don't go, Father, over the mountains.'

But her father would ask her why she is afraid, and she would not know what to say. So she sits in silence at the door of their shack and watches him leaving with his quick steps.

One day she asked him.

'What is behind there?' she said.

'Earth,' he replied. 'Earth and people.'

'Many people,' he said, 'with great houses up to the sky.' When she grows up, she will go to see them.

But little Avgi has no curiosity about people and great houses, for the sea is beside her. It is not the open ocean. In the distance are the lines of islands, and among the islands are openings where the sea runs without end and meets the line of the horizon. Avgi can make her dreams travel through these openings and be happy. She sits on the seashore, plays with the pebbles and touches the breaking waves with her hands. Then she is sure that her message will be taken by the waves to the other end of the ocean, through the openings in the islands. And since the sea has no end, neither will this journey.

When winter comes with its rains, Fotis does not go to the fields but sits all day long with them. Vaso, his new wife who came from the border of Iran, has grown used to the sea-people and to the sea. She sits at the window of their shack and looks at it indifferently, without fear, while Fotis tells his children, tells Avgi, strange things about a distant place they came from. There the earth was blessed and gave a hundred times what you sowed, and the people lived restfully and peacefully until they died.

'Why do we not go there again?' Avgi asked.

But her father did not wish to reply. He merely said, 'Now we will put our roots down in this land and we will work the earth and it will give us a hundred times the seed we sow, like the earth of the place we came from.'

But to Avgi it remained inexplicable why, if they had such blessed earth in the other country, they had to suffer and dig this dry land.

When the rains passed and spring came, Avgi sometimes went with her father to the fields. The dark vines spread before them in endless rows, bare and leafless, and the heart of the little girl clenched from sorrow. She had seen them in the summer adorned with green leaves, and now she thought that some great evil must have come for them to be so bare.

They won't become green again, she thought.

She remembered then the dead fish the fishermen threw into the sea from their boat, when they were cleaning the nets. Avgi remembered how they sank slowly, without strength to move like the living fish she saw when she leaned over the edge of the mole. She said it would be like that: 'The dry vines will be like the dead fish.'

For, without their leaves, nothing in them moved. They had the stillness of death.

When Fotis went to the field of the little god, where Eleni was at rest, Avgi always followed him. They went together to the tomb, which was nothing but a bucketful of soil raised on the surface of the earth.

'Cross yourself,' her father would say. 'Your mother is under here.'

Avgi crossed herself fearfully and wished there was a way of seeing her mother's face under the earth.

Mostly, her memories of her mother were faint. But she did remember vividly the hands that had caressed her. Oh, how well she remembered them! For since the time that the water had taken her mother, Avgi had not felt the same caress. Of course, there was her father and her new mother, Vaso. But *her* touch was different.

Avgi, therefore, would like to dig up the earth until she found the buried hands. But, when she ventured to say so one day to her father, he replied quickly that it was impossible, for the hands and the body of people become earth.

So while her father dug the field beside her, whistling, Avgi sat alone a long while on the tomb, taking fistfuls of earth and holding it until it became warm. Then she put it back carefully from where it came.

THE END

MODERN
GREEK
CLASSICS

C. P. CAVAFY
Selected Poems   BILINGUAL EDITION
Translated by David Connolly

Cavafy is by far the most translated and well-known Greek poet internationally. Whether his subject matter is historical, philosophical or sensual, Cavafy's unique poetic voice is always recognizable by its ironical, suave, witty and world-weary tones.

STRATIS DOUKAS
A Prisoner of War's Story
Translated by Petro Alexiou
With an afterword by Dimitris Tziovas

Smyrna, 1922: A young Anatolian Greek is taken prisoner at the end of the Greek–Turkish War. A classic tale of survival in a time of nationalist conflict, *A Prisoner of War's Story* is a beautifully crafted and pithy narrative. Affirming the common humanity of peoples, it earns its place among Europe's finest anti-war literature of the post-WWI period.

ODYSSEUS ELYTIS
1979 NOBEL PRIZE FOR LITERATURE
In the Name of Luminosity and Transparency
With an Introduction by Dimitris Daskalopoulos

The poetry of Odysseus Elytis owes as much to the ancients and Byzantium as to the surrealists of the 1930s, bringing romantic modernism and structural experimentation to Greece. Collected here are the two speeches Elytis gave on his acceptance of the 1979 Nobel Prize for Literature.

NIKOS ENGONOPOULOS
Cafés and Comets After Midnight and Other Poems
BILINGUAL EDITION
Translated by David Connolly

Derided for his innovative and, at the time, often incomprehensible modernist experiments, Engonopoulos is today regarded as one of the most original artists of his generation. In both his painting and poetry, he created a peculiarly Greek surrealism, a blending of the Dionysian and Apollonian.

M. KARAGATSIS
The Great Chimera
Translated by Patricia Barbeito

A psychological portrait of a young French woman, Marina, who marries a sailor and moves to the island of Syros. Her fate grows entwined with that of the boats and when economic downturn arrives, it brings passion, life and death in its wake.

STELIOS KOULOGLOU
Never Go to the Post Office Alone
Translated by Joshua Barley

A foreign correspondent in Moscow queues at the city's central post office one morning in 1989, waiting to send a fax to his newspaper in New York. With the Soviet Union collapsing and the Berlin Wall about to fall, this moment of history would change the world, and his life, forever.

ANDREAS LASKARATOS
Reflections
BILINGUAL EDITION
Translated by Simon Darragh

Andreas Laskaratos was a writer and poet, a social thinker and, in many ways, a controversialist. His *Reflections* sets out, in a series of calm, clear and pithy aphorisms, his uncompromising and finely reasoned beliefs on morality, justice, personal conduct, power, tradition, religion and government.

MARGARITA LIBERAKI
The Other Alexander
Translated by Willis Barnstone and Elli Tzalopoulou Barnstone

A tyrannical father leads a double life; he has two families and gives the same first names to both sets of children. The half-siblings meet, love, hate, and betray one another. Hailed by Albert Camus as "true poetry," Liberaki's sharp, riveting prose consolidates her place in European literature.

ALEXANDROS PAPADIAMANDIS
Fey Folk
Translated by David Connolly

Alexandros Papadiamandis holds a special place in the history of Modern Greek letters, but also in the heart of the ordinary reader. *Fey Folk* follows the humble lives of quaint, simple-hearted folk living in accordance with centuries-old traditions, described here with both reverence and humour.

ALEXANDROS RANGAVIS
The Notary
Translated by Simon Darragh

A mystery set on the island of Cephalonia, this classic work of Rangavis is an iconic tale of suspense and intrigue, love and murder. *The Notary* is Modern Greek literature's contribution to the tradition of early crime fiction, alongside E.T.A. Hoffman, Edgar Allan Poe and Wilkie Collins.

EMMANUEL ROÏDES
Pope Joan
Translated by David Connolly

This satirical novel and masterpiece of modern Greek literature retells the legend of a female pope as a disguised criticism of the Orthodox Church of the nineteenth century. It was a bestseller across Europe at its time and the controversy it provoked led to the swift excommunication of its author.

ANTONIS SAMARAKIS
The Flaw
Translated by Simon Darragh

A man is seized from his afternoon drink at the Cafe Sport by two agents of the Regime by car toward Special Branch Headquarters, and the interrogation that undoubtedly awaits him there. Part thriller and part political satire, *The Flaw* has been translated into more than thirty languages.

GEORGE SEFERIS
1979 NOBEL PRIZE FOR LITERATURE
Novel and Other Poems   BILINGUAL EDITION
Translated by Roderick Beaton

Often compared during his lifetime to T.S. Eliot, Seferis is noted for his spare, laconic, dense and allusive verse. Seferis better than any other writer expresses the dilemma experienced by his countrymen then and now: how to be at once Greek and modern.

MAKIS TSITAS
God is My Witness
Translated by Joshua Barley

A hilariously funny and achingly sad portrait of Greek society during the crisis years, as told by a lovable anti-hero. Fifty-year-old Chrysovalantis, who has recently lost his job and struggles with declining health, sets out to tell the story of his life, roaming the streets of Athens on Christmas Eve.

AN ANTHOLOGY
Rebetika: Songs from the Old Greek Underworld

BILINGUAL EDITION

Translated by Katharine Butterworth & Sara Schneider

The songs in this book are a sampling of the urban folk songs of Greece during the first half of the twentieth century. Often compared to American blues, rebetika songs are the creative expression of people living a marginal and often underworld existence on the fringes of established society.

AN ANTHOLOGY
Greek Folk Tales

Translated by Alexander Zaphiriou

Greek folk tales, as recounted throughout Greek-speaking regions, span the centuries from early antiquity up to our times. These are wondrous, whimsical stories about doughty youths and frightful monsters, resourceful maidens and animals gifted with human speech, and they capture the temperament and ethos of the Greek folk psyche.